Dracula's Diary

Dracula's Diary

Michael Geare
& Michael Corby

BUCHAN & ENRIGHT, PUBLISHERS
LONDON

First published in 1982 by
Buchan & Enright, Publishers, Limited
21 Oakley Street, London SW3 5NT

ISBN 0 907675 06 9

Photoset in North Wales by
Derek Doyle & Associates, Mold, Clwyd
Printed and bound at
The Pitman Press Ltd, Bath

Preface

This Diary was discovered by its editor in unusual circumstances.

As a writer he always needs change and holiday, and is generally too poor to pay for it. His holiday last year at Mrs Bobescu's Boarding House in Angst in Romania was therefore on a negotiated basis, with a reduction for washing up, bed making and henhouse duties.

It was in the course of the last named that he found, giving inadequate support to a roosting box, a pile of bound notebooks: their contents were seen, astonishingly, to be written in English, and subsequently proved to be the actual Diary of the renowned Count Dracula.

How it came to be there is not known. Mrs Bobescu's aunt, Mrs Lupescu, indicated – as well as toothlessness and a cleft palate would allow – that they had been placed in their supporting position at least twenty-five years ago. The ravages of time (the Diary appears to have been written during the 1870s), weather and the natural functions of Romanian roosters had inevitably wrought some havoc on the great Count's entries (in this connection it is particularly regrettable that some sections dealing with Dracula's English sojourn at Eton and Balliol have been lost through defecation, for it is likely that Dr Jowett was no less powerful a formative influence than the towering figure of the Count's uncle, Prince Vlad).

If Mrs Bobescu proves amenable (and if this Diary sells well) the editor hopes to return to Angst to search for further records of Dracula's later career.

September 15th

It is my eighteenth birthday, and over breakfast I received my presents. Biro, my personal servant, has given me cartridges for my wildfowling piece; Mr Drummond, my English tutor, a cricket bat; my Uncle Vlad sent me a beautiful ivory ornament representing a dozen recently severed heads on poles, and my dear Father has given me a handsome book, *The Good Blood Guide*, with a note 'My Beloved Son, in his 18th year, must read and discuss this with me carefully'. (It is probably a sort of supplement to the *Almanach de Gotha*.)

For the past two years Mr Drummond has read to me at mealtimes; the Brontës for breakfast and Dickens for dinner, but I was let off as a birthday treat. I must say that over the past several months I've been enjoying bacon, eggs and sausages much less, and rather craving for underdone steak and Buda-Pesth Blood Pudding, but this was a jolly meal. Dear Biro, who has quite a gift for drawing, did a caricature of me as I sat: for some reason we don't have any mirrors in our Castle, but I seem to be quite good-looking, really, except for rather pronounced teeth.

My dear Father wasn't at breakfast, but then he never is. I believe he is engaged on some great scholarly book, for he seems to work all night and then sleep all day in his bedroom in the basement, which he keeps very private. He has been looking unusually well lately – sometimes he appears rather gaunt – and as there has been a specially good harvest in the estates round the Castle, and hundreds of cheerful young peasant girls have been brought in to help with the harvesting, it has been a particularly happy time.

Later. How dreadful that a day begun so happily should become so sad. (From now on I shall write in this Diary only at the end of the day.) While I was enjoying my elevenses, there suddenly arose an awful crying and keening in the great courtyard outside. A dreadful sense of foreboding seized me, and I pushed away my honey syllabub untasted and sat trembling.

Soon our major-domo Mikhail – he is the sixth of the Footescu family to serve us – came in. He is white-haired and very tottery nowadays, but generally voluble if incoherent. Now he said, very quietly and simply, 'Young Master, your Father is dead.'

I will not dwell on my fearful sense of grief and loss. It was Mr Drummond who rose to the occasion: he lit his meerschaum, struck me hard on the shoulder, saying, 'Play up, Dracula, play up and play the game', sent messengers post-haste to my Uncle Vlad, and pieced together what had happened to my beloved Father.

It seems that he went for a walk after dark. One of the peasant girls, terribly pale and drawn, confirmed that she had seen him and he had indeed kissed her (basically my Father had a most affectionate nature). He must then have lain down, probably to contemplate the glorious harvest moon.

During the day the permanent peasants had been re-fencing the grazing fields. Our bailiff, a bookish man called Andreas Deutsch, had given each of them a work quota: one of them, Hoch by name, had fallen so far behind that Andreas had sent him out to complete his quota by moonlight. My Father must have been lying in a patch of shadow: the wretched and unobserving Hoch – I can hardly bring myself to write this – had inadvertently driven a stake, not into the earth but right through my Father's heart.

To bed, sick with sadness.

September 18th

Mr Drummond and Biro have been a wonderful help to me in the last two days.

Mr Drummond said I must keep a stiff upper lip: he looked me closely in the face and added, rather cryptically, 'You shouldn't have too much difficulty.' I've always wondered how such a perfect Englishman came to speak our Central European languages so well, and he explained that his father had spent much time in the service of the great Austrian Chancellor, Prince Metternich, helping to put down liberalism. 'My father was greatly against all wishy-washy liberals and social democrats. He was very tenacious; indeed, our family nickname is Bulldog.' He is a fine man, and he has promised to teach me fast underhand bowling at cricket to take my mind off things.

Biro also made a cryptic remark. He said: 'I know everything about your Father and the Draculas, but he saved my life and I will serve you until death.' It seems that Biro, who is about three years older than me, was one of the happiest little boys in Transylvania until his mother died and he got a new young stepmother who was terribly cruel to him. 'She was beautiful and full-blooded and she thrashed me fiercely every day and twice on Sabbaths. Then your Father came and saw her: he came several times and in a month she was dead. So when I was older I begged to see your Father, and said that, in gratitude, I wished to serve the Draculas all my days. So here, young Master, here I am.'

It is good to have such friends.

September 21st

Just before dawn I was woken by a great clatter: Uncle Vlad and his entourage had arrived. He is the undisputed head of our family; the great Prince Vlad, revered and feared. I didn't wait to remove my nightcap, but rushed down to welcome him. He looked as fierce and reassuring as ever.

'My dear boy,' he said, hugging me, 'we'll talk about this dreadful tragedy at supper tonight. The sun will soon be up, I've had a hard journey, I'm off to bed.'

'Old Footescu said he knew exactly the arrangements you'd want.'

'Hope he's got them right. Wouldn't want to impale the old dear,' said my great Uncle briskly. Then he added, 'You, young Dracula, d'you still get up and about in the daytime?'

I said, 'Yes, of course,' puzzled by his tone, and he grunted and went off.

I must now confide in this Diary that, as well as an increasing desire to eat food with blood in it, other strange feelings have been coming over me. I'm aware of being increasingly sluggish and uneasy by day, especially on the brilliant sunny days that we get in the Transylvanian autumn, and then as dusk falls and my bedtime approaches I'm increasingly alert and active. Further, when I see some pretty peasant girl my member – which I had thought was only there so that I could relieve myself – becomes engorged and greatly expanded.

I told Mr Drummond about this phenomenon some time ago. He was reading and memorising a new English publication called *Whitaker's Almanack*: he laid it down, carefully relit his pipe, and said, 'Don't worry, dear boy. I'll get your Father to talk to you about the Facts of Life.'

'You're my tutor. You're the one who tells me all the facts.'

'Not those of Life,' Mr Drummond said quite severely.

But after that he made me run twice round the Castle and have a cold tub every morning before breakfast and *Jane Eyre*. Alas, my poor Father will never now have the chance to tell me these Facts.

What I didn't tell Mr Drummond about this engorgement (he said in an unusually quiet voice that I might describe it as an erection) is that it is accompanied by a similar distension of my eye teeth: the upper gums at that point on each side of my mouth seem to swell so that the two teeth are forced downwards. As far as I can feel, they extend four or five centimetres below my lower lip. This is very confusing and embarrassing, and the only advantage is if it happens when I'm shaved. (Biro and Mr Drummond tell me I have raven-black hair and a strong growth of dark moustache and whisker, and the latter soon gave me one of his cut-throats to keep me 'looking regimental'.) But it's particularly easy to shave an upper lip that's stretched and pulled tight.

September 22nd

An evening with Uncle Vlad. What a marvellously vital person he is. Even before supper – at which he seemed to eat very little – he had been out in our estates, and said he had made contact with one of the workers. He was in fine form and, about midnight, had my Father's killer, Hoch, ritually impaled before a large audience. Hoch shouted a good deal – I suppose impalement is really quite painful although I don't suppose the workers feel it as we would – and there was a tremendous amount of applause and celebration: I don't think he was a very popular peasant.

Uncle Vlad was in two minds about impaling Andreas Deutsch as well. Finally he ordered him to leave the country with his family that night; he added cuttingly, 'I suggest you put your heirs and successors to deal with books rather than with real people.'

September 24th

A very solemn night. In the Castle's great cellar Uncle Vlad conducted a most moving funeral service for my Father. There were innumerable candles, the ceremony lasted a long time, and when the great coffin was finally sealed and carried out I was deeply moved. So was Mr Drummond, although he was rather bewildered by the various dignified rituals: 'It's a bit different from evensong in Godalming,' he said.

September 27th

Uncle Vlad and Mr Drummond get on extremely well, and tonight we played three-handed whist together, a game we all enjoy. Suddenly Uncle Vlad said, 'Drummond, what are we to do with this excellent boy? I've got to get back to my estates: can't leave him here on his own, not even with you. What do you suggest, eh?'

My tutor puffed at his pipe several times – I remember he blew a perfect smoke ring that hung still in the air above the candelabra – and then made a momentous suggestion.

'He could come to England, and be finished as an English gentleman. After that he is secure anywhere in the world. As a member of a distinguished European family, my dear Prince, Dracula would have no difficulty in entering Eton, then Balliol, and then spending some time in London as a young man about town. I'm very fond of Dracula, he's made of the right stuff, and I should make it my duty and pleasure to keep an affectionate eye on him.'

There was a long silence. The candles guttered as we awaited my Uncle's decision: I hardly know whether I hoped for his consent or refusal. Then he cried, 'By God, Drummond, that's it! Put in a couple of bailiffs to run the place. And when young Dracula returns, a man of the world, there'll be nothing he can't do. What is the first step we should take, Drummond?'

'Teach him to box,' said my tutor calmly. 'I shall arrange for the British champion, Henry Brute, to come out here immediately.'

October 4th

Mr Drummond went back to England today. He has much to arrange, finding me a place at a public school and an Oxford college and setting in hand the purchase of a London house. We shook hands with a long firm grip before he sprang into the calèche and started off down the arrow-straight drive to the Castle gates, over a league away. I cannot deny that a tear sprang to my eye, and Biro was in the same case, as we are both deeply fond of our admirable Englishman. From all that he has told me and given me, I know that I shall be very happy in England, the greatest country in the world.

October 6th

Uncle Vlad spent the day deciding on the joint bailiffs to administer our estates — which are enormous and stretch far beyond the Borgo Pass. The quality of applicants has not been as high as we hoped — my Uncle with his sense of brusque fun said he'd had to get rid of a lot of Wallachian wets (he impaled one candidate who foolishly said he'd never work a seventy-hour week) and mouldy Moldavians. He has finally settled on two men from the Buda-Pesth area, Niklaus and Tomas, who appear confident if unattractive.

'Have your supper early,' said my Uncle. 'I am going to tell you about our family, the Szekelys, and about your life and future. It will be a long hard night.'

So it was with a clench of apprehension that I saw him enter the room as I finished my frankfurters, for although I love my Uncle I also fear him. Biro rose and disappeared as if with foreknowledge of something momentous.

Uncle Vlad sat in silence for a few moments, opened the casement windows wide, muttered gruffly to himself. 'So much to explain'; and began: 'Dear boy, do you believe you are exactly as other men?'

The question stirred the odd feelings and forebodings that I've lately experienced, but I only replied, 'Well, I am much richer and better connected than most.'

'You are more. You are much more,' Uncle Vlad cried in a great voice. 'You are one of Us, and we are Vampires. We are the Un-Dead. After we leave our teens we survive only by sucking blood, by drinking blood, from living men. Or better,' Uncle Vlad added with a rasp in his throat, 'from living maidens.'

I would have fainted at this fearful revelation had I not, in some small way, almost expected it.

'It is hard being Un-Dead. Sometimes good blood is difficult to find and we grow gaunt and sad; we may even have to hibernate in a coffin filled with our native soil. Our eyes increasingly cannot endure the light of day or sun so that we must work and play at night. We have many allergies, to Christian ornaments, mirrors and garlic, for example. But we have great strengths, too.'

'Tell me,' I said, but more strongly as I felt my wits returning.

'Follow,' he cried, and strode to – and out of! – the window. When I peered out anxiously he was crawling down the Castle wall, face first and with his long cloak tucked in his belt. Apart

14

from wheezing a little, for my Uncle is prone to touches of asthma, he seemed utterly secure.

'Follow,' he repeated fiercely. 'You can do it.'

To my amazement I found that indeed I could, and I crawled up and down the Castle face for some minutes. When we were both returned to the room my Uncle said: 'I told you. Did you enjoy it?'

Mr Drummond has impressed on me the importance of truthfulness, and indeed I had no alternative. 'I fear I did not. I had a terrible feeling of vertigo, of nausea. Perhaps I shouldn't do it on a full stomach for – you must excuse me – I'm going to be sick.'

As I rushed from the room I heard him call, 'I will show you more of our Powers tomorrow night.'

October 9th

I supped very lightly, not knowing what the next Powers might be. The day had been calm, for it had come almost as a relief to know everything; to be able to talk with Biro about it, for he has hitherto kept his knowledge to himself.

My Uncle burst in. 'Right, dear Dracula,' he shouted, 'think of bats.'

For a moment – for the good Mr Drummond had been teaching me to square cut only a few minutes before he left –I thought of stories of the English cricket field, but my Uncle's fiery eyes were on me, and I thought of *Die Fledermaus*, which the Bukovina Amateur Operatic Society had given earlier in the summer and which I had rather enjoyed. My Uncle's blazing eyes were close to mine.

'Say, "Change, change, change"; repeat "I am changing to a bat, to a bat ..." '

As we chanted together, his eyes grew smaller, his body shrank, I watched bewildered as he became a bat: then I looked

15

down at my own body and *so had I*!

We flew northwards, making a wide arc over the cattle byres, sheepfolds, pigsties and wolf pens. I have to say that I felt no sense of great release. I raised my ears and uttered a few squeaks but certainly could not share my Uncle's apparent pleasure in the exercise. And there was a fearful whizzing sound when some great brute of a bird – I think it was a barn owl – swept up from nowhere and took a nasty peck at me.

Back in the room and in our usual forms, my Uncle demanded, 'Did you like *that*?'

'Alas,' I replied quickly, 'I seem to have a Fear of Flying. I've neither head nor stomach for it and must beg you once more to excuse me. I'm going to be sick again.'

October 10th

It was a very taciturn Uncle Vlad who joined me this evening.

'Right, Dracula,' he said shortly, 'it's wolves tonight.'

I was not myself in the best of moods as I'd had to sleep on my face: the owl's peck at my anatomy had made this a painful necessity.

We went through broadly the same procedures as for bats, and quite soon were loping together past the asparagus beds towards the wolf pens. I've never really liked our wolves, and when we reached the pens I liked them even less and was reminded how noisy and how smelly they are. (What with Mr Drummond making me take cold tubs and hot baths all the time, and clean my teeth six times daily with Dr Calvert's English tooth-powder as he says I might have a tendency to halitosis, I'm rather fastidious in this area.)

Uncle Vlad lifted the outside latch with his muzzle and the wolves came out, howling and chattering, with white teeth, lolling red tongues, long sinewy limbs and shaggy hair. I had expected at least a degree of respect because of my Uncle's

16

commanding presence. But he quickly disappeared in their midst and some of them came up to me, sneering and jostling.

'That's a wretched-looking specimen.'

'Must be a teen-age werewolf.'

'Couldn't frighten a sick grandmother.'

'Couldn't catch a broken-down droshky.'

There was a torrent of similar, jeering remarks as the wolves hustled and shouldered me. Suddenly I became very angry. I don't say that I wasn't frightened — all my four knees were knocking together — but I remembered what Mr Drummond had said in our preliminary boxing lessons and I flew straight at the nose of the largest and roughest wolf and sank my fangs in. It was evidently extremely painful, for when he finally managed to shake free — I held on tenaciously — he whimpered rather pathetically and then laid his muzzle in a pile of cold entrails, as a kind of poultice, I suppose. The other wolves backed away very respectfully, and I was still feeling quite pleased with myself as we changed shapes outside the moat gatehouse and strolled back to my room.

As we entered it, my Uncle clasped my hand in a violent grip. 'My dear boy, my dear Dracula,' he cried, 'my faith is restored. When you were so timid with the crawling and the flying, I began to doubt you. "Is he a true Szekely or a mere milksop?" I asked myself. But when you rounded on that great wolf, Casanova, then I knew that all was well, that your heart was in the right place.'

We shook hands again, very warmly, and I went to bed happier than I had been for some weeks.

October 14th

Last night Uncle Vlad set off for home. Before he left he told the new bailiffs, Tomas and Niklaus, that I would soon be going to England, that they would have charge of the great estates, and that if they failed in their duties he would have them impaled; very slowly. They replied that he need have no worries as their economic theories, however unconventional, were profound, proven and rooted in Hungarian soil.

Uncle Vlad said to me: 'Now I know you have the blood and the heart of Szekely. Soon you will return with the armour of an English Gentleman. You will make the name Count Dracula yet more famous, to the furthest corners of the Carpathians.'

He turned away, and said with some embarrassment, 'There is one other thing I must tell you; something very curious. There lives in London a collateral branch of our family; Roy and Shirley Dracula. But they wrote to me some years ago saying that they were lapsed vampires and that they had undertaken a new and congenial occupation.'

'What would that be?'

'I only know that it is something to do with an English politician, a Mr Peel, who has invented something called Income Tax. They collect it.'

'But you told me ...'

'Indeed, if we vampires fail to take in living blood, we enter into a death-like catalepsy. If they have lapsed they should be in that state. And yet ... and yet ... such is the communication between the Un-Dead that I would know if they were. It is very strange and rather disturbing: I thought I should tell you of it.'

I was emboldened to ask, 'Can we be killed absolutely? Are not the Un-Dead well-nigh immortal?'

He rounded on me, his face suddenly old with sadness. 'How can you ask that,' he said angrily, 'with your beloved Father even now growing warm in his grave? Of course we can be killed absolutely: it is far from easy for our enemies to end our

18

existences, but they have often contrived it over the centuries.'

I longed to ask more questions, but his fierce grief showed that my Uncle was in no mood to answer. Then in a quick gesture he laid an arm affectionately across my shoulders and we embraced.

As he and his outriders disappeared into the night the wolves cried, and tears came to my eyes; my faithful Biro clasped my hand sympathetically.

October 15th

As a compensation, a calèche this morning brought Henry Brute with a portmanteau which proved to contain messages from Mr Drummond, Mr Brute's garments, a number of boxing gloves, and innumerable bottles of scent, which this champion prize-fighter applies lavishly to his person. Biro and I think it has a strong and disagreeable odour, but the wolves seem to like it.

Mr Drummond's letters inform me that he has found a suitable house for me to buy, so that I may have a London home. He had at first considered a large property near Purfleet, called Carfax, but decided that the twenty-acre estate was too large and gloomy. Finally, however, he decided that No 347 Piccadilly would be admirably central, well placed for London's club land, well suited to my needs. He has arranged for a Mr Jonathan Harker, of a solicitor's firm called Hawkins, to come here within the next week or so to give me full details of the property and the contract and to take back my necessary signatures. He ends by enjoining me to 'remember the overriding importance of a straight left'.

October 16th

Mr Brute is quickly at work – he insists that I call him 'Enery – and in my first day of light sparring, as he calls it, he has worked me harder than did my fencing master.

October 20th

At the end of a week I am delighted with 'Enery, who is as merry as a grig and very painstaking and clearly a wonderfully experienced boxer. I think he is quite pleased with my progress, for I certainly enjoy the lunge and riposte, the punch and counter-punch. I am even getting used to the terrible perfume that he pours over himself. All the servants, including Biro, are his slaves, but I am a little concerned that the Castle's three serving girls. Trandafira, Vlastimila and Pavola, are *quite* so slavish.

October 22nd

'Enery was in reminiscent mood today. I can now understand the strange sort of English that he uses and, after a session on slipping the left leads, he gave me a fascinating talk on combination punching and footwork. I realised that 'Enery could have been a — rather massive — ballet master.

November 1st

Rather a difficult day. After some enjoyable sparring, Mr Harker arrived in a calèche. He is, I think, a rather junior member of the firm of English solicitors, and this appears to be the first time he has tasted freedom — or slivovitz. I find this pungent plum brandy rather disagreeable, but Biro drinks it, and so had Mr Harker — in quantities.

November 2nd

Although Mr Harker was in a rather tremulous state, we discussed the Piccadilly purchase and I signed the necessary documents. The invaluable 'Enery will take them back to Mr Drummond when he leaves at the end of the week. I am very pleased with him and feel I now know how to defend myself like an Englishman (I've requested Mr Drummond to pay him above the agreed fee).

I asked what he thought of my progress.

'It's like this, young Count,' he said, 'you ought to be a natural: lovely footwork, lovely mover, nice timing. 'Ard for the other bloke to lay a glove on you. I could even teach you combination punching. Trouble is, though – I 'as to be frank – there's no power in your punches: wouldn't dislodge the skin from a rice pudding, not the 'orrible thick ones my missus makes.'

I was downcast at this and after supper confided my worries to Biro. He said nothing for a while and then, as if coming to a crisis of resolution after a long-pondered problem, he fixed his eyes on me above the unsteady candles (the snow was gusting against the Castle casements) and spoke with great intensity.

'Young Master, you cannot deny your destiny. I know that you are of a race of vampires: I see you so weak, and I know why. You must have blood. Young Master, it is life and strength to you and you *must* have it.'

I recoiled. 'I've no taste for it, Biro.'

'Taste or no, it is your destiny. And you must accept it: accept it *now*. Begin tonight; become a bat as the illustrious Vlad showed you; take blood from Trandafira, Vlastimila and Pavola; take a little from each and in the morning they will have bites in the neck and feel a little fatigued, nothing more. And,' Biro added sharply, 'what with that 'Enery, at present they're quite used to that.'

I felt an awful indecision. 'It will do them no lasting harm?'

21

'It is only if you constantly return to them that they will join the Un-Dead. An occasional draught from them does little injury. Indeed some leeches and physicians recommend it.'

Still I was undecided. The candles' flames masked Biro's earnest face from me; I made to move the great silver candelabra — I could barely pick them up! With both hands, so weak had I become, I could only with difficulty raise them.

'Biro,' I cried in my frustration, 'I'll do what you suggest. I'll do it tonight.'

November 3rd

Such a day! I duly transformed myself — as far as I could tell I closely resembled a *Desmodus rufus*, of which there are large numbers hereabouts. After midnight I made my way to the scullery bedroom, above the old torture chamber, and did what was necessary. The girls hardly stirred, but I must say that as I looked at them, tumbled and part naked in the snowy moonlight, a kind of fibrillation in my bat's body suggested that there might be something further that I should do: I resolved again to ask Mr Drummond about this when we are re-united in London.

But I must record the effect of this seemingly essential draught. 'Enery and I had a farewell sparring bout. Knowing the lightness of my blows he was scarcely troubling to defend himself so that I was able to hit him flush in the face. He went over like a jack rabbit! I don't know which of us was more delighted: there were tears of happiness in his eyes as well as blood on his nose.

'I can go back to London, 'appy,' he shouted. 'You 'ave a real punch as well.'

November 8th

Biro and I greatly miss 'Enery, although not as much as do our three serving girls. (They seem totally unaware of the contribution they had made to my renewed vigour, although Pavola did complain that it was funny to be bitten by mosquitoes during snowy weather.) Our great concern now is Jonathan Harker. He must have brought a great many bottles of slivovitz in his luggage, and is somehow replenishing his supplies, I suspect through Janos Paislic the gravedigger. He is a huge, hideous man with a terrible voice: much as I dislike him I cannot have him dismissed or killed since, inexplicably, he was a great favourite of my beloved Father.

Harker, on a constant intake of this ferocious spirit, seems in a permanent state of hallucination. He rambles on about wolves, and about seeing creatures creeping down the battlement walls (I have, in fact, had a practice crawl, but that was on the north-east face, where he couldn't possibly have seen me). He also makes strange remarks about Trandafira, Vlastimila (who are brunettes) and the blonde one, Pavola: their laughter is 'like the intolerable tingling sweetness of water glasses', they are 'honey sweet' and have 'a deliberate voluptuousness which is both thrilling and repulsive'. We now learn that on his way out – he came via Munich – he had to be rescued after some kind of breakdown near the tomb of the dear Countess Dolingen of Gratz in Styria.

He also talks a good deal about a young woman called Mina Murray to whom he appears to be affianced. She sounds to be a harmless enough young woman and gifted at working the typewriter: I can only hope she will be happy with Mr Harker.

November 30th

We leave tomorrow. We are going to Varna to pick up the Orient Express to Paris and thence to London. Mr Harker is certainly in no state to travel with us. Tomas and Niklaus, the new bailiffs, have therefore undertaken to get him to the Hospital of St Joseph and Ste Marie in Buda-Pesth; Sister Agatha there has a reputation for rehabilitating cases such as his. Tomas and Niklaus agreed rather grudgingly, and only after I had reminded them of Uncle Vlad's predilection. I told them the story of when my dear Uncle had indulged in some heavy impaling of malcontents at his summer folly and – until they realised the futility of it – the local police kept sending officers to him 'to pursue enquiries'. Uncle Vlad fed them all to the wolves – until the wolves protested that all those large uniform buttons were playing havoc with their teeth!

The two bailiffs did not join Biro in his hearty laughter: they are glum, arrogant men but, I suppose, skilful economists who will make our vast and rich estates yet more profitable. Tomas said sourly, 'Respected Count, you will understand our basic economic principles. The augmentation of the nominal value of produce is not necessarily enhancing to the net value given, *ceteris paribus*, that the marginal propensity to consume is inversely related to marginal price which can be taken as an income substitute. Now, given the non-stable equilibrium induced by the marginal demand for giffen goods, we see the solution is to increase the gross disposable income of the factors of production hence increasing the marginal propensity to consume on the one hand while eliminating the surplus value on the other.'

After a fairish pause I said, 'Of course, eliminating the surplus value'; and left to watch Biro packing our extensive belongings for England.

December 3rd

After the excitements of the long railway journey it is wonderful to be in London, reunited with Mr Drummond in his rooms in Half Moon Street. After Castle Dracula they seem, of course, rather small; but then so does my property nearby at No 347 Piccadilly, although Mr Drummond tells me that by London standards it is unusually commodious.

December 8th

Dear Mr Drummond has done so much. All is organised at Eton and he will take me down and introduce me to the Provost, Dr Charles Goodford and the Headmaster, Dr James Hornby, at the beginning of the Hilary term. He has concluded the purchase of the Piccadilly house and engaged a butler who will take on the other staff. I quite liked the butler, Horrolds, on first meeting but Biro says he has shifty eyes and bad teeth and that he wouldn't trust him a centimetre. Mr Drummond has also put a notice in the *Morning Post*, saying that Count Dracula is in England and temporarily resident with him.

December 9th

This morning we put on the gloves or, as Mr Drummond prefers to call them, the mufflers. He took his pipe from his mouth and we sparred for some time: he is delighted with my progress under 'Enery.

'Such footwork and timing,' he said. 'Of course, if we were really boxing you'd have a much stronger punch?'

'It seems to vary with my diet,' I said cautiously (Biro kept very still).

'Quite so, quite so. I'm sure that I've heard of some fighting

25

sailor who has to have spinach to bring him up to strength.'

Despite all this, Mr Drummond still made me have Swinburne for supper. 'Don't like the chap,' he said. 'Nasty rumours about him. But he went to Eton, and these *Poems and Ballads* are supposed to be hot stuff. So I'm afraid you'll have to read 'em.'

December 10th

No doubt it is partly my bewilderment at the size and noise of London, but I have been feeling increasingly unwell during the day. I don't think it can be London alone since – unlike poor Biro – I have seen the sophistication of Buda-Pesth and am certainly not overawed, even though I am in the mightiest capital in the world. In the evenings and at night I feel extremely well, fascinated by all the talk of war and politics and affairs – for Mr Drummond seems to have a considerable entrée, and has quickly plunged me into soirées and dinner parties. I am excited by the brilliance of the gas lights, the endless rattle of landaus, phaetons and broughams (some with formidable rear spikes to deter children from taking rides), omnibuses and innumerable tradesmen's carts. I find the smell of horse dung disagreeably pervasive at times – but am much more concerned by my growing allergy to the full light of day.

Mr Drummond is worried about this daytime lassitude, and says he will take me to his physician, who is particularly helpful and goes in for what he calls deductive diagnosis, a Dr Watson.

December 16th

I feel that I am adjusting very well to my greatly changed life – although of course a European nobleman can feel some confidence anywhere in the Old World. I am not sure about America from what I hear of that new country (but Uncle Vlad once told me that they are very sound in their treatment of Indians). Apart from my growing discomfort in daytime, I have settled in very well to the size and strangeness of London, and am looking forward quite calmly to the new experience of going to Eton College next week. Mr Drummond, who does not give his approval lightly, has congratulated me on having an old head on young shoulders. 'In a year or two's time,' he said, 'when you are both a Transylvanian aristocrat and an English gentleman, you may be able and willing to do some service for both countries.'

He said this one evening when one of his friends was there, a good-looking man called James Stock. Stock is a wonderful cards player – we were playing three-handed whist – and seems to travel a great deal: he is also fussy about his drinks, insisting that his punch 'must be stirred, not shaken'.

There is something a little mysterious about them both, and I have a feeling that although Mr Drummond is very rich (not of course by my standards), he *does* something. It might be occasional work for the British Government, perhaps in the educational field. And he seemingly visits two ladies whom I have not yet met: he refers to them as Phyllis and Kay.

But, while he was out this evening seeing Kay, I had another tremendous shock. Biro announced two callers: 'A Mr and Mrs Roy Dracula are here to see you, Master.' This visit was so momentous that I must wait till tomorrow to write fully about it.

December 17th

This must be a lengthy entry, for my talk with Shirley and Roy may prove of the greatest significance.

First of all they asked after Uncle Vlad.

'It's just a hundred years since we saw him: he was younger then, and such a dear man.'

'A hundred and ten,' said Shirley.

'Surely a hundred, dearest. We saw him at that wonderful Walpurgis Night family reunion — that was ten years before we left and we've been here just ninety years now.'

Shirley made some calculations on her fingers and said nothing.

'Do you remember how we bought those two chests of our native Transylvanian soil from Brasov? Such a comfort they were to us.'

'To you,' said Shirley shortly. Then she asked me earnestly, 'Do you know about yourself and the Dracula destiny? Are you — are you practising?'

I outlined to them the extent of my knowledge and experience, and then asked with the most intense interest, 'But what about you two? Uncle Vlad thought you were alive but lapsed. Can vampires lapse? Please, please tell me everything: I *must* know.'

There was a pause, then Shirley said, 'You tell him.'

'Right-ho,' said Roy, settling himself very deliberately. 'It all began when we decided to come to England and start a new life —'

'It was his idea, and for the first fifty years it was a great mistake. I told him it would be but he never listens. We thought the quality of English blood was bound to be better, but it wasn't. I was chronically malnourished, I tell you, and then there was snuff.'

'Shirley has an allergy to snuff,' said Roy mildly.

'All through the Regency time I suffered from snuff: the women were as bad as the men and I got quite ill with asthma.

28

For years it was a wretched, neck-to-mouth existence.'

'But tell him about the better times, my dearest one. My idea when Sir Robert Peel invented Income Tax.'

'It was *my* idea. I said if we can get blood out of people better than anyone in the world, then why not money? Why not work for the Income Tax people?'

Roy clipped a cigar and said, 'We discussed it together carefully ...'

'I decided we'd do it. But the first problem was how to work in daylight. You can't do a regular job if you can't even work in daylight.'

'You, my dear Dracula, are already beginning to find difficulty with daylight, and you're only about five per cent, or perhaps 6¼ per cent, through your life,' Roy interposed.

'So I had a stroke of genius. Dark spectacles. Roy, put on your dark spectacles for Dracula.'

Carefully, he took out an elaborate case, and placed on his nose a pair of spectacles seemingly made of a thick, dark green glass. I had never seen such things nor dreamed that they existed. I cried out, 'Can I, then – can I obtain such things?'

'Easily,' answered Roy, 'we'll introduce you to such a nice man, really our family physician now. You mustn't be worried if he has occasional odd turns. His name is Dr Jekyll and he lives —'

'Later, later,' said Shirley impatiently. 'Our next problem was even more pressing. And I solved it. Roy, show him.'

From a pocket in his tailcoat Roy gingerly extracted a square, dark red bottle. I examined the label eagerly. It said: HAEMOZADE. The Blood and Iron Tonic. As Used by His Excellency Count Bismarck.

He handed the bottle to me. 'Available at all good London pharmacists. 2/9d the large size.'

'I solved it just like that,' continued Shirley. 'We take a full glass nightly, and we're no longer dependent on blood. An occasional topping up ...'

'And you know, dear heart, I think I almost prefer claret now.'

'Don't interrupt,' said Shirley crossly. 'You and your German wines. Anyway, that's how I saved the situation; that's how we lead quite normal lives, that's how we've – I suppose you must call it that – we've lapsed.'

'Perhaps, heart's own,' said Roy, 'we should tell him about the earlier ...'

'No, you tell him if you must. I'm going to tidy my hair.'

As this was clearly very necessary, I called for Biro to take her to Mr Drummond's bathroom. Roy lit a cigar, and I gave him a glass of Mr Drummond's Marsala which he appeared to enjoy.

'Actually,' he said, 'it was somewhat earlier that I stumbled on a similar Mixture. I used to have my hair and whiskers trimmed by a little man in Fleet Street. He seemed to have one or two sidelines: he was in a sort of pie business with some dreadful female, and he produced, specially for me, I think, this kind of mixture that met our needs very well. Todd's Tonic, he called it. Shirley's rather sensitive about it in view of what happened to poor Sweeney; but, anyway, these Haemozade people took over where he left off.'

'It's better?'

'Even better. And –' he lowered his voice, 'I think it's the Iron or Steel or something in it – it makes me look at girls in quite a different way: Shirley doesn't approve at all.'

I leaned forward to ask Roy if he would develop this theme as it was of considerable interest to me, but various banging noises indicated that Shirley had finished her *toilette* in the bathroom, and was having a good look round Mr Drummond's flat.

Roy sighed, 'Such a dear girl. She does like to know about everything. Now, Dracula, if I were you I'd lay down a gross of the stuff immediately.'

December 18th

I rose early and ordered a gross of Haemozade from the chemists in Wigmore Street, paying a surcharge for immediate delivery. My mind is still reeling from the happy implications of Shirley and Roy's revelations: what a delightful man he is. We have of course exchanged addresses.

January 6th

Entered Eton today. Mr Drummond introduced me to the Provost, the Headmaster, and to Dr Joynes, a well-known master. Biro came down here a few days ago and has taken comfortable lodgings in Keate's Lane. He says that Dr Joynes has a reputation as a bircher, even of older boys: we both laughed at the idea of anyone birching *me*.

I thought that Eton looked very flat, but Mr Drummond took me up in his kind way. 'Has to be flat to have good playing fields. Remember, but for these fields, the Battle of Waterloo would have been lost, and we would all have been under the heel of the Corsican Ogre. He might well have suppressed the *Morning Post*, cricket and boxing.'

Mr Drummond has always encouraged me to argue with him.

'Did not the Prussians really win Waterloo?'

'Their general,' he replied unperturbed, 'a brave fellow called Blucher, actually believed he was pregnant by an elephant.'

'Would that, then, be very difficult?'

Mr Drummond refilled his pipe, using his thumb a good deal. 'My dear Dracula, we have touched on this theme before. I take it that in no way did your respected father acquaint you with the – with what we call the Facts of Life? Or even your excellent Uncle Vladimir?'

He seemed less assured than usual: I felt that I could hardly tell him the Facts that Uncle Vlad had imparted to me.

'No,' I replied.

'Oh, dear. How awkward: that's not really my department.'

Mr Drummond's tanned features seemed to have taken on a richer colour. Then he struck his forehead with his large hand: 'I have it. I know the old tutor of the Prince of Wales. He had to explain this Aspect of Life to his Royal Highness, and everyone agrees that he did so with quite extraordinary success. I shall arrange for you to meet him. At the end of this term he shall come to your Piccadilly house and – and, well, talk to you.'

March 6th

I have not kept a day-to-day entry of my first term here, and shall not do so. I have a purpose here, and I strive to fulfil it, attending classes, working hard. I believe the masters think I am a model pupil, my fag that I am a model master. I am certainly well liked in Williams's Bookshop, where I am an excellent customer.

Different as they are from me, my admiration for the English grows. They have a great sense of fair play, are surprisingly eloquent (but only in English) and have a supreme sense of confidence: it causes me no surprise that these young men go forth and govern colonies or rule great tracts of India; that they become officers in a navy or an army, for ever sending gunboats or winning battles against tribesmen, fuzzy-wuzzies or even Abyssinians. The ordinary people whom I see in London and in Eton seem to live much better than do the people in my native Transylvania, perhaps because they have not for centuries lain under the malignant shadow of the Turks (Biro and I cannot understand how the English went to war, how even clever Mr Disraeli nearly went to war, with Russia to help those terrible Turks, but perhaps that was part of Disraeli's cleverness).

Biro tells me that some of the people who come from the new industrial towns, which have what Uncle Vlad calls dark angelic mills, look less well; skinny, with bad colour and teeth and looking as if they had suffered from rickets. But the Army and the Navy seem to make smart brave men out of them.

March 8th

Among the particular friends I have made are young Roberts and the Hon. Crispin Bell-Mountain: both are destined for the Army, and the former's father is already rather famous – a veritable *sahib bahadur* in the Army in India. I go quite often to Bell-Mountain's House, and know his Housemaster, Mr Walton, and Mr Walton's daughter, a fair, well-developed, full-blooded girl called Erika.

She is such a bold girl that it is hard to believe that she has only recently left the tutelage of Miss Beale at Cheltenham College for Ladies. Bell-Mountain, whose father is concerned with the recently formed Rugby Football Union, declares ungallantly that she'd make a fine rugger forward. Forward she certainly is; she appears to find me attractive since, whenever she has the opportunity, she comes and sits next to me – very closely.

Strangely, I also find myself attracted, with a return of the curious manifestations of which I have written earlier. I eagerly await the end of term and the promised revelation by HRH's retired tutor of the mysterious Facts of Life.

March 10th

Whilst I am on excellent terms with all the men here, there is one exception. He is called Hooley, a big bullying chap with a loud voice and heavy eyebrows, who has seemed to resent me from the start.

I was strolling past the new Physical Science School, lost in thought over a new scientific proposition which had just been explained to me, when I bumped heavily into somebody: it was Hooley.

I will not write down how offensive he was: certainly he hurled even more abuse at me than I had received during my experience in the wolf pen. I listened with mounting fury; then, removing my invaluable tinted spectacles and staring icily at him, I said, 'If you ever speak to me like that again I shall thrash you within a centimetre of your life.'

He looked as if he would burst: indeed the shoulder seam on his jacket did.

'*You* thrash *me*!' he roared. 'You bottle-glass four-eyed upstart! You —' he groped for a word of ultimate abuse – 'you *foreigner*.'

He went on, 'And when would you like to administer this thrashing? Now – d'you think – now ...' and he began tearing off his already torn jacket.

I thought decisively. I couldn't fight in my dark green glasses; if I took them off I would quickly feel unwell and not do myself justice. Besides, although the Eton diet plus ample supplies of Haemozade were keeping me perfectly fit, I was sure that to develop my best punch – the right uppercut that had so bowled over my dear and unsuspecting 'Enery – I needed something better than a substitute. And in a flash I divined an admirable substitute for the real thing.

'Right, then, Hooley,' I said crisply. 'I won't brawl with you now. I will fight you in the gym tomorrow night at dusk. Bell-Mountain will be my second: he will arrange for the ropes to be put up and the light mufflers to be available. I take it you are not afraid of this proposal?'

He replied, with a good deal of illustrative detail, that he was certainly not afraid, and stumped off to tell his friends.

I went to Bell-Mountain's House, and he expressed every willingness to do as I suggested. He said, I thought with some lack of conviction, 'I'm sure you'll be all right, old fellow. He's a great, strong, heavy bruiser, but I expect you'll be too quick and clever for him.'

After a brief reconnaissance, I returned to my rooms for a few hours of valuable sleep. In the clear light of cold fury I knew exactly what I had to do during the hours of darkness.

March 11th

I slipped out at 1 a.m. Although all was dark and silent there was a fitful moon and I thought the risk of being seen wandering the Eton streets was too great, so I transformed myself. Not into a bat – after the episode with the barn owl (and from its nocturnal noises I suspected Eton to be full of owls), I've thought it risky to be a bat out of doors – but into a wolf.

I loped along easily enough, and was almost at my destination when I ran into trouble – trouble in the form of an enormous Alsatian which had no right to be out at that hour. The last thing I wanted was a fight with a dog in the morning, with Hooley in the evening. However, it soon appeared that the animal's intentions were not violent but amorous.

'Go away,' I said, 'I'm not a normal dog.'

'Nor am I, duckie,' he replied in rather a piping voice, and leaped at me.

Fortunately I evaded his rush, and while he was re-organising himself I very quickly, and with some difficulty, transformed myself into a bat and flew hastily to the window in Walton's House which I had identified as being in Erika's bedroom. The casement was ajar, I scrambled in thankfully, and transformed myself back to human form.

I tiptoed across the dark chamber towards the sleeping figure in the bed. I was surprised to find that it was snoring loudly – so loudly that some ornament on the mantelpiece was vibrating in response – and distressed that a girl so ripe, so feminine, who had so oddly touched in me deep, uncomprehended feelings, should make such a peasant's noise. And then I started back – not in fear, for we Draculas do not accept fear – but much disturbed that the shafting moonlight had revealed, near to her pillow, some small, awful, fanged ectoplasmic thing. This brought me in contact with an aspidistra, which I judged from the noise it made in falling to be one of the biggest in the world. At the crash Erika sat up in bed, thrust her hand into the ectoplasmic thing, and

35

cried, 'Burglars! Felons! Where are my teeth?' in a voice so bass that I realised I had misjudged the room.

With singular speed I changed my form, shot out through the window of what was Erika's father's bedroom and – since there were several owls hooting and honking nearby – flew through the adjoining casement. At that juncture I coined for myself a highly appropriate phrase, which roughly translates into English as 'going like a bat out of hell'.

But my troubles were far from over: Erika evidently slept with an oil lamp lit in her room, her father's bellowings had already aroused her as well as dislodging a small glazed china pig, and when she saw me – before I could utter a word or a squeak – she screamed, 'A bat! A bat! My hair! My hair!'

She leapt from her bed and rushed into a small adjoining room. She was wearing a long woollen nightdress, yoked and delicately embroidered at the throat, but it did not disguise the fineness and fullness of her figure. Even as I thought admiringly of this I was forced to admire her spirit too: she emerged from the little room grasping a long-handled, stiff-bristled brush, used for cleansing the inaccessible parts of lavatory pans, and pursued me round her bedroom lashing out at me and crying, 'You shan't get in my hair, you brute, you.'

She was wonderfully vigorous and accurate, and I blessed the moment when her father rushed anxiously into the room, leaving the door open and enabling my escape into the corridor.

I hid behind the head of what appeared to be a rather disgruntled elk (could not help thinking that our Transylvanian taxidermists would have done better) until, when they had decided that the aspidistra must have toppled over from its own considerable weight, calm was restored.

'I'm going to take a sleeping draught,' said Mr Walton crossly as he stumped back to his bedroom.

I transformed myself again, tapped lightly on Erika's door and instantly entered. She was sitting in bed reading *Oliver Twist*; she looked up and her eyes widened with astonishment, but she made no sound. Instead, she slipped silently to the door and bolted it.

Then: 'Oh, Dracula darling,' she whispered, 'I'd so hoped – I'd hardly dared to hope – that *you* would be the first. I've hardly been able to wait for It to happen – and now It will happen with you.'

I was decidedly confused at this, and my confusion grew worse when she suddenly seized me in her arms and – she really is an unusually strong girl – threw me on her bed, kissing me very energetically and inaccurately and wriggling about a great deal. I felt that strange surge of central warmth and tumescence to which I have alluded in this Diary, but above all I was instantly able to kiss her strongly and repeatedly in the neck: a flood of strength and power overtook me as I took in this marvellous ichor. I do not think she even noticed, such was the intensity of her excitement.

After a while I relaxed my embrace and rolled back, feeling marvellously fulfilled. She looked at me, her eyes questioning and amazed. 'Is that It? There must be more to It than that?'

I was wondering what to answer when she went on excitedly, 'I know; of course I know. You are keeping yourself till after your fight with that horrible Hooley. You must beat him' – I assured her that I would – 'and come back to me tomorrow night, my triumphant hero.'

I said, 'Yes'; and wondered what Uncle Vlad would have said.

'My brave, darlingest Dracula,' she went on in a rush, 'it will be wonderful tomorrow night. I used to talk about It with my friend Fiona in the dorm at Cheltenham Ladies' College. She got quite plump and had to go for a holiday in Switzerland, but she's just back, in Windsor, and I shall talk to her tomorrow. I know she knows all about It, and we'll have the most wonderful, wonderful time in the world tomorrow night.'

The clock in the corridor struck a reluctant three. 'And now, my gallant knight Dracula, you must go.'

We tiptoed downstairs, she let me out with a brief '*A bientôt*' and a prolonged kiss, I changed and loped home, chasing two tomcats en route from sheer exuberance, and was sleeping soundly when Biro woke me with coffee and croissants. He looked surprised when I declined my Haemozade.

Hooley and I squared up in the gym just after dusk. The news of the fight must have been bruited around, for many boys were there and there was a great buzz of excitement. Hooley, stripped to the waist, proved to be a well-muscled young man: he must have outweighed me by some ten kilos. My second, Bell-Mountain, put on a brave front and made a great business with his bucket and sponge, but I sensed that he was very worried. I retained my silk singlet, which led to some suggestions of effeminacy, but as Hooley was liked only by his cronies, the general feeling appeared to be of hope that I would win, of near-certainty that I wouldn't.

He attacked me from the very start, landing a series of thumping blows: my forearms and upper arms upon which (following 'Enery's teaching) I received all the punches I did not evade felt quite tender and bruised. At the very end of the first round I hit him once with a crisp left jab. As he awaited the opening of the second round he glowered at the crowd, which was humming with pleased surprise, and dabbed aggrievedly at his nose, which was bleeding.

As we came up again he renewed his attack, but this time so wildly that my opportunity was clear. I hit him twice: a straight left followed by a right cross – and there he was flat on his back.

'Out for the Count!' screamed Roberts (I thought this an excellent if accidental joke), and then everyone was around me patting my back and applauding. Nobody was taking much notice of Hooley, although Bell-Mountain, more I fear in derision than from any desire to revive him, emptied our bucket of water over his head.

When the plaudits were over and Biro had proudly buttoned up my snowy shirt, my hand was suddenly grasped and warmly shaken. It was Hooley – I felt a sharp twinge of sympathy as he had all too evidently lost a tooth – and he said, 'Well done, Dracula. Real bite in your punches. Absolutely first class.'

I wonder if I will ever understand the English.

Back in the lodgings Biro gave me an unusual drink – he said

it was champagne and Haemozade and he called it Red Velvet —
and I faced him squarely.

'Have you ever done — done It with the peasant girls?'

'Of course, Master.'

'Then please tell me, and in detail, about It.'

March 12th

Soon after midnight Erika and I were reunited. She had left the
front door on the latch ('Darlingest, it was so romantic of you to
climb up the ivy last night — but suppose you fell, where would I
be?'), and in no time I was in her bedroom, where she removed
her yoked nightgown and my silk underwear with speed and
deftness; the combined instructions of my Biro and her Fiona
seemed technically adequate: I found It a rich and enjoyable new
experience.

So, I am sure, did she. Indeed, after a pleasantly exhausted rest,
she rolled over, whispered, 'Little me is a little like Oliver
Twist'; and straddled me. I lay back and thought of
Transylvania.

As, just before dawn, we slipped quietly down to the front
door (although her father's regular snores, like a summer
thunderstorm rolling over the Carpathians, made extreme silence
unnecessary) Erika gave me a tremendous farewell hug. Then she
whispered: 'It was marvellous, marvellous, marvellous! But
darlingest Dracula, you forgot to give me any love bites in my
neck tonight. Don't forget next time.'

This morning Biro dispatched an electric telegraph message
from me to dear Mr Drummond: 'Pray do not now trouble
Royal tutor as Facts now revealed.'

April 4th

It is pleasant to be back for the school holiday in my own house in Piccadilly. Despite his teeth, Horrolds has done excellent work; all is clean and elegant and cheerful (old Footescu, our Castle Dracula major-domo, could profit from a visit here, but I fear the journey would knock the stuffing from the dear old scarecrow). I like the staff he has taken on – with one exception, Mrs Marster the housekeeper. I find her manner vulgar – and *her* teeth put me in mind of some Gothick horror tale. Horrolds looked alarmed when I said that she must be replaced immediately, pleading that she was an admirable woman and an excellent typewriter as well. But I was adamant, remembering indeed that the wretched Harker's fiancée was also reputed a fine typewriter, which hardly equipped her for other duties.

'Horrolds,' I said, 'I am going on Tuesday to stay for a week with my Eton friend Bell-Mountain at Cotterell Castle near Chipping Stoat in the Cotswolds: his father is the Earl of Cotterell. By the time I return Mrs Marster must be gone and another housekeeper installed.'

He said nervously that he would try to get her employment in some lord's house.

April 5th

Judge my surprise when, of all people, Harker appeared here today accompanied by his new wife, Mina the typewriter. He looked unimaginably better: it seems that at the Hospital of St Joseph and Ste Marie they had put him on a strict regimen, with nothing stronger to drink than goat's milk, and, after some while, his affianced Miss Mina had herself gone to Buda-Pesth and collected him. 'I tell you, Count Dracula,' he said earnestly. 'Sooner than drink that Slivovitz again, I'd drink methylated spirits.' I thought a shade of unease moved over Mina's face.

After Harker had thanked me for my kindness (and when I thought what Uncle Vlad would have done with him, I *had* been kind) he explained the purpose of his visit.

'I very much hope' – he was too abject for my taste – 'that despite my unfortunate lapse you will continue as a client, a greatly valued client, of our firm. And of course the costs and responsibilities of my recent marriage to my good lady here mean that we're glad of all the work we can get.' He simpered at Mina, who didn't simper back.

I was about to return a discouraging answer when a twinge in my loin reminded me of Erika. I said, 'Harker, pray find and purchase for me at a suitable price a small apartment, a *pied à terre,* in central London suitable for a single person of either sex to spend a few days in.'

He shook my hand profusely, assuring me that he would instantly attend to it. Mina – unless I am very greatly mistaken – Mina *winked* at me. Indeed, she winked twice.

April 7th

The train from Paddington to Charlbury was exactly on time (railways seem to have wonderful standards of punctuality and service which I suppose they will never lose, certainly not in England), and there was my good friend Bell-Mountain waiting at the station in a smart chaise.

'Told the coachman I'd meet you myself,' he said exuberantly as he drove off at a spanking pace. Dogs, cats, peasants and sheep all leaped out of his way, and in no time we were through the lodge gates and up the long straight drive to the great building, which still has its moat and commanding pele. My spirits, already high, were lifted at seeing a castle rather resembling my own beloved Castle Dracula.

'Don't worry, old fellow,' cried Bell-Mountain, 'it's not as primitive as it looks. When my father inherited years ago he got a funny little architect chap, Tom Hopper, to re-do it, y'know.

41

Once you get out of the Great Hall, which looks like Winchester Cathedral and is shocking cold, it's a very comfortable place.'

April 16th

Safely back in Piccadilly after a most interesting week, I hasten to record my impressions and recollections.

Bell-Mountain himself took me to my room; very comfortable with a bright coal fire.

'Should tell you,' he said. 'This room is supposed to be haunted. It's a Cavalier, I think, with gouged eyes and a blood-soaked face. The pater tells me several guests have seen it and left in a hurry: one lost his wits. Became an MP later, I think. Don't suppose anyone who can thrash the bully Hooley will worry about a ghost.'

To my amazement, on the very first night, after a good dinner with excellent Warre's port, an apparition appeared and woke me up. I jumped from my bed, looked him full in the eye sockets and smiled as widely and pleasantly as I could. I was feeling decidedly scared, when the awful apparition suddenly gave a hoarse, terrible groan.

'It's the evil Un-Dead! It's not English. Unfair, unfair, unfair to phantoms.' He moved in a panicky way across the room, smashing a Haemozade bottle (fortunately I had a spare) and disappearing up the chimney: I was relieved that the fire was by then a mere ember. He did not return for a further conversation.

Another night was rather different. There were several younger people among the Castle party, Etonian friends of Bell-Mountain and myself, and some local country girls. One of these was called Amanda Rice-Todhunter, apparently a scion of a Cotswold military family. I found myself riding with her one morning, and at dinner she paid the greatest attention as I told her about Carpathian bloodsports. In the small hours I was awakened by this young woman standing at my bedside in a flowered robe.

'What on earth are you doing?'

'The same,' she replied, 'as everyone else in this damned castle.'

She then removed 'her robe – despite the draughtiness of the corridors it was all she was wearing – and bounded into my bed. What followed was agreeable, refreshing and put me much in mind of Erika.

Another episode was far less pleasant. The Earl was extremely fond of baccarat, and after dinner a game began in the smoking room. Amongst the players were the Hon. Arthur Holmwood and a friend of his, a Dutchman called Dr Van Helsing – I have to say that I took an immediate dislike to both of them.

To be brief, it became apparent that Holmwood was cheating, in that he was adding to his stake after the cards were declared in his favour. A terrible scene followed, of which I was a witness, with Arthur Holmwood declaring that he was playing the baccarat system of 'coup de trois' (by which the stake is increased threefold after every winning coup); Van Helsing supporting him; everyone else disbelieving him. I realised that although the English remain admirably unmoved by battle, murder and sudden death, they regard matters such as cheating, shooting foxes and dynamiting fish with the deepest concern.

General Rice-Todhunter, my agile Amanda's father, was brought in: he and the Earl rapidly prepared a document for the Hon. Arthur's signature under which, in return for secrecy, he undertook to give up the playing of cards. Holmwood looked up as he was protestingly signing this document, and his eyes seemed to hold mine longer and more bitterly than they held the others': I felt I had made an enemy.

I wondered why the Hon. Arthur should seem to hold a special resentment against me. I had certainly tried to disguise my instinctive revulsion to him and his crony, Van Helsing, although we Draculas seem to have a special perception of those with evil natures and powers.

Later I asked Amanda if she could think why (she too was in slight disgrace, for tobogganing down the main staircase on a large tea tray – 'They do it at Sandringham,' she said rebelliously, 'why not here?'). 'Well,' she replied to my question, 'if word of his cheating gets out, Arthur's done for socially. He thinks the English will keep mum; doesn't know about you, you being a Continental.' She went on, 'Dracula, dear, it's our last night together in this house – do we have to have all these blankets? It's like a load of earth on top of us.'

April 17th

An interesting development in Piccadilly. Horrolds has replaced Mrs Marster with a very agreeable woman, Mrs Merry. Her only fault is a fearful tendency to speak in doggerel: when first introduced to me she curtsied and said,

'I'm sure that you will be a fount
Of kindness to us, honoured Count.'

I am therefore avoiding any prolonged conversations with Mrs Merry, much as she radiates goodness and amiability. But I am getting very little sympathy from Biro who has instantly fallen headlong in love with Pamela, Mrs Merry's daughter. In her parlourmaid's uniform she looks extremely pretty – if common – with blonde hair and an excellent development, and Biro has been exercising his real talent for drawing by making innumerable sketches of her. He also has a talent for languages – since we went to the Eton lodgings we have spoken only English together – and as he evidently sees Mrs Merry as his future mother-in-law he has begun to imitate her doggerel conversation. For example he got a glimpse (accidental, I trust) of Pamela undressing and reported to me that:

'She loosed her garments outer
Presenting to my happy eyes
Delicious thews and lovely thighs
And bosom like a pouter.'

44

April 28th

I return to Eton tomorrow. Mr Drummond and James Stock came round: after supper (we had a delicious Eel Broth) we played cards and Mr Drummond said, 'You were down at Cotterell's place, Dracula, when that business happened of Arthur Holmwood cheating?'

'I don't think I should say anything about that. It's all being kept secret.'

'Then it's the worst-kept secret in the world. London's buzzing with it: Holmwood will have to resign from his clubs, the Marlborough and the Turf. I tell you, it could hardly be more talked about if the Prince of Wales himself had been involved.'

Stock said quietly: 'Your reticence is of course quite admirable and proper. Tell me, though, did not Van Helsing, against all the evidence, support him?'

'He certainly supported him.'

'What was your opinion of Van Helsing?' Stock asked.

'I didn't like him. He was very loquacious: he speaks English fluently but like a foreigner –' they both laughed at this and after a moment I joined in – 'but he somehow seems to me a sinister person.'

As they were leaving, James Stock made two curious requests.

'Could you consider taking up a rather interesting hobby – I think you've got the right kind of brain for it and I'll send some books to you – the study of Codes and Ciphers.'

Puzzled, I assented, and he added: 'And also, could you practise eating a little paper every day?'

'Eating *paper*!' I exclaimed.

'Yes. Don't start with anything indigestible like *Truth*: something easy like the *Morning Post* or *The Times*. But just make sure you can eat and swallow it easily.'

Mr Drummond and Stock exchanged glances, and Stock went on, a little defensively, 'I think it's important. I was talking to young Strickland last night – he's just finishing his furlough from

45

India – and he reminded me of its importance.'

'I shall be most grateful if you will do what James asks,' said Mr Drummond gently, so of course I agreed. Just when I think I am beginning to understand the English.

August 2nd

I have now completed two halves at Eton, and will go up to Balliol in a couple of months' time, at the beginning of the Michaelmas term. I have learned a great deal here, and made many friends especially in my second term since, after thrashing Hooley, I really seemed to be something of a – if the word is not too fanciful – a legend. I feel that I know the sons of at least a half of *Burke's Peerage and Baronetage*. Some of their grandparents apparently remarked that my bout had a better end than that in 1825 when Ashly died after a fight of over 60 rounds.

I cannot say that I feel any regret at having played neither the Field nor the Wall Game: the latter appears to me grubby, foetid, undignified and pointless. But I've much enjoyed my cricket – a game far removed from politics and approaching the realms of philosophy. I had two encounters which I particularly remember; in each case when watching a match after having enjoyed a satisfactory knock.

A very pleasant young man came up and said energetically: 'Liked your batting, Dracula. Very stylish indeed. Good wrists, good eye. Keep your cricket up, won't you. Take it back to Transylvania.'

He told me his name was George Harris, and that he'd played for Eton against Harrow in 1869.

'What did you score?'

'A duck.'

'Oh, dear, I suppose that spoiled your chances. Who do you play for nowadays?'

'Nowadays,' he said, strolling away, 'nowadays I captain England.'

He wandered back to me a little later.

'Y'know, Dracula,' he said, 'great thing about cricket, it could be universal. I mean, you're a foreign feller — very English foreign feller, of course, but still foreign. Technically, I mean. But you're enjoying cricket: everyone can enjoy cricket, all colours and everything. Tell you, they can turn practically everything else in the world into some damn political issue. But not one will ever be able to bring cricket into politics.'

The other meeting was with a strange shock-haired man, in his forties I supposed, who came up to me after I had scored a satisfactory 64, mostly on the off side, in a trial game (I'm proud to say I was in the XI against Harrow as a result).

'You're a very clean-limbed player, Count,' he said, rather quickly and nervously. 'May I introduce myself: I'm Swinburne.'

'Swinburne the poet?'

He shuffled his feet and beamed assent.

'Mr Drummond, my old tutor made me — I mean, he and I have read your *Poems and Ballads* and greatly enjoyed them.'

'Good, good. Now tell me, what do you think about birchings and floggings, eh?'

I couldn't recall witnessing any, but he went on. 'I watched a great many when I was a boy here in the 1850s. I've written a great many poems about it all —' his eyes grew very hot and bright — 'like in "Reginald's Flogging"':

To feel once more the red rod plied amain
And writhe and smart and burn and tingle with the pain.'

I have this dislike of violence so I said nothing.

'Or in "Rupert's Flogging",' he went on eagerly,

'Swish. Fiercer the master's dark eyeballs grown now
Than the eye of a dragon is
Each schoolboy is thrilled by the sight of his
Bare-bottomed schoolfellow's agonies.'

47

As I considered the rhyme, I thought it would be dangerous to bring my Mrs Merry and Mr Swinburne together.

'Were you flogged?' I asked apprehensively.

'Oh yes, oh, yes. By several people, especially the Rev. Joynes.'

'You mean our new Lower Master?'

'Yes, indeed, he. He was my tutor; I lodged with him; I hated and despised him. I wrote a poem about him. Would you like to hear it?'

'I'm afraid I have this rather delicate stomach —'

'No, no, no. This isn't a flagellation one: its a despising one. It goes:

> Dully and dumbly the depths of thy dimness
> Drown and depress the dear delicate days
> Thy lymphatic lump lies like leaded and limbless
> Lumber that limits all laughter and lays.
>
> Permitted perhaps is your poor pedant's prosing
> Pale and precise as a python in pain
> But thy sharp stinging snatches, thy sour soul exposing
> Such —'

At this point (rather resourcefully) I dropped my cricket bat on his instep and he ended the recitation. I had feared that it was going to get nasty again.

When he had finished hopping about, Swinburne asked, without malice, I think, 'Are you returning to Transylvania when you leave Eton?'

'Indeed no. Mr Drummond and I are in correspondence with Balliol, and I hope to go up to that College for the Michaelmas term.'

'Splendid, splendid,' cried Swinburne. 'If you do not know the Master, Dr Jowett, pray allow me to introduce you personally. Dr Jowett is a dear and close friend of mine.'

I thought this unlikely, but when I looked sceptically at Bell-

Mountain who had just joined us (he had sat on his stumps after making 2: not alas a natural cricketer) he nodded firmly to indicate that this really was the case.

September 15th

Swinburne proved as good as his word, and today, my birthday, took me up to Oxford to see Dr Benjamin Jowett.

Bell-Mountain, when I told him of the projected visit to Balliol, said, 'You'd better watch Swinburne: he's not only a poet but he's rather a cad as well. Dr Jowett has called him the oddest of Balliol's children. I ask you.'

'His father was a British admiral.'

'I know, I know. But, well, there's something else the pater told me.'

'Then please tell me, Bell-Mountain.'

'Well — it's what the pater said — he said something about flagellant brothels.'

It is evident that neither of us knows much about flagellant brothels, but I have made a note to enquire of Uncle Vlad, who is bound to be knowledgeable in this field.

When Swinburne and I reached the Master's Lodging, he and the Master indeed greeted each other very warmly. Dr Jowett has a large forehead and a small pursed mouth and at first looks more like an English country parson than an academic so famous that someone (surely not Mrs Merry) has written of him:

'First come I, my name is Jowett
There isn't knowledge but I know it.'

He was very agreeable and asked me questions. 'Tell me, Count, do you write poetry?'

'Yes, Master,' I replied. 'Perhaps not as well in English as in my native tongue, but, for example:

Upon the softly crested hill
The evening sun declines and stays
An instant, casting still
Its dusted tangent rays.'

'Good, good,' said Jowett, nodding vigorously. 'Burn it, burn it.' (I took his advice earlier this evening.) He followed this up with further valuable guidance, and I have noted down three of his comments.

'Write something everyday if you mean to write well.'

'Look to poetry and literature rather than the barren fields of metaphysics.' (I warm to this advice.)

'When you come up, six hours' study a day will get the best out of you.' (I feel less enthusiastic about this.)

As I shook hands on leaving, he gave me some advice that I'm sure will be treasured and followed: 'A good sort of roguery is never to say a word against anybody – however much they may deserve it.'

September 16th

With Eton behind me – although I hope often to return – these few weeks in my Piccadilly house before I go up to Oxford should be very agreeable. Mr Drummond and I are well pleased that my education as an English gentleman is so well begun: many friends made, especially Bell-Mountain. He is kind, devoted, very well connected and not overwhelmingly bright – an ideal friend.

And then there is Erika. Harker has been unexpectedly competent in purchasing for me a small, discreet dwelling in New Row, just off St Martin's Lane. I had to leave the furnishings to him and, since they appear entirely adequate, I suspect that his typewriter wife Mina has had a hand in these arrangements. Erika, therefore, can come – does come – to London 'to stay with friends', and we meet there most happily.

Since she positively demands that I 'nibble her neck' I always leave these conjunctions feeling like a giant refreshed. She is of course a bold and independent girl, but I have to record that Mr Walton, her widower father, allows her far more freedom than I would ever give to a daughter of mine.

During my last weeks at Eton, except when the demands of cricket inevitably took precedence, I visited her regularly, and she was much affected by her romantic belief that I always scaled the ivy (which looked thoroughly unsafe to me) to reach her casement. She will never know how nearly that infernal lavatory brush ended our romance. And perhaps my life – though there are physiological family details here which I must discuss with Uncle Vlad.

September 18th

I have been in two minds about returning for a visit to my Castle: a detour would enable me also to see my dear Uncle. But I have been kept so regularly and fully informed by Tomas and Niklaus that it scarcely seems necessary. I recall that I found their personalities arrogant and unattractive, but they have proved assiduous in giving me frequent and glowing reports – albeit written in an astonishingly clumsy style – of the progress of their plans and the mounting prosperity of the estates, that I evidently misjudged them. Almost from the beginning the envelopes of their letters were instantly identifiable, each bearing a little decoration in the similitude of a clenched fist.

I suppose I could discuss a possible return to Castle Dracula with Shirley and Roy, who after all are kith and kin. Yet I hesitate to do so, or indeed to discuss the affairs of the family with people so long sundered from them. I am becoming very fond of Roy, however, in spite of his inroads on my claret, but I find Shirley's breathless indecision and untidiness decidedly unattractive:

'A nest of robins in her hair
My eyes declare they could be there.'

Thus did I overhear Mrs Merry comment, and I see just what she means.

There are some lacunae *in the Diary over this period. There is evidence that the Count gave less attention to his journals whilst at Eton and Balliol; also, these sections suffered the most from the unfortunate, if natural, attentions of Mrs Bobescu's fowls. The next entry is dated almost a year later.*

September 17th

As at Eton, so at Balliol, I am concentrating on my work. I keep in trim with cricket and boxing, but realise that I can look forward to a very long life indeed, and intend to be properly educated and equipped for it. I have no enemies here, but if some of my contemporaries think me reserved and stand-offish, this occasions me no distress. Nor do the broader themes of Oxford today greatly interest me: the building of the new Examination Schools; must Greek remain a compulsory requirement of an arts degree, or why is Paley's *Horae Paulinae* now out of use.

I read a great deal during the vacations, and my study in the Piccadilly house already contains a large library. I went on one reading party to the South of France but had to return early as I was made quite ill by the pervasive smell of garlic. I went also to one of Dr Jowett's West Malvern reading parties. He told me firmly, 'Always read the best poets and keep up a habit of regular attendance at church': the former instruction I follow; the latter is, to say the least, difficult for the Un-Dead.

But during the vacations I do a great deal more than read. I go much to the theatre (Biro goes to the music halls, sometimes with his Pamela), to many society balls (for I am an excellent dancer, my waltzing being especially admired) and I play baccarat in moderation. I stay regularly at Cotterell Castle, shooting and hunting with my dear friend Bell-Mountain: it is always delightful to renew my acquaintance with the beautiful Cotswolds, and also with the delightful Amanda Rice-Todhunter from Chipping Stoat (although in general I remain rather faithful to dear Erika). I box sometimes, at Ned Donelly's School behind the Café Royal. If it is possible, I have become even fonder of Mr Drummond, who has introduced me to his clubs and many of his friends; and cousin Roy Dracula and I meet regularly as well.

I was dining at one of Roy's clubs, the Marlborough (of which Arthur Holmwood is *not* any longer a member) when he introduced me to a well-known poet, Alfred Austin. When I told him of Dr Jowett's advice about my own verse he was extremely interested.

'I'm sure, Count,' he said earnestly, 'that you'll enjoy the long poem which I now have in preparation. It's a marvellous panoramic survey of Our Island History from Elizabethan times to the present day. It's very fatiguing work, of course, and needs immense research. I expect you'd like to hear one or two couplets.'

Roy said that we would, at the same time signalling to a club servant for another decanter of port.

'Now, Sir Francis Drake must be a significant early figure. So I've written:

Across the wide expanse of Plymouth Hoe
Drake's balls he gallantly did throw.'

'Very good,' we both murmured.

'It is, it is. I think it exactly catches the vivid swashbuckling nature of the period. Then, after the Cavaliers and the Roundheads, I move on to an effective dying fall:

It seemed that Civil War might last for ever
But Charles's head they finally did sever.'

The poet brushed a tear from his eye. 'It's very affecting, is it not?'

We agreed that it was, and Roy took a large swallow of port in a way which suggested – not quite truthfully, I thought – that the verse had overwhelmed him emotionally.

'Then, as we come into this century,' Alfred continued, 'I deal with the great figures, Nelson and Wellington:

The waves that swept across great *Victory*'s decks
Lord Nelson's corns most grievously did vex.'

'Very fine,' we said.

'Yes, indeed. I thought long about that subtle touch: the great man, the hero, yet afflicted with the same ordinary weaknesses as his own men.'

Roy took out a notebook and made an entry. Alfred looked extremely gratified at this although a quick glance over Roy's shoulder showed me that he had written 'Remember – get Corn Plasters from Chemist.'

'But I have a different touch with Wellington. Here we are:

Across the rolling fields of Waterloo
The Duke declared "the Froggies shan't get through".'

I think you'll agree, the word "Froggies" is an inspired touch. Wellington's whole character is there.'

'Have you finished this noble poem?' I enquired.

'No. I have about sixty glorious years still to go. And I must complete and dedicate it very carefully. You know,' Austin added roguishly, 'poets *can* be peers nowadays.'

'Indeed. Lord Austin would sound just as well as Lord Tennyson.'

'We shall see. We shall see. Glad you so greatly enjoyed my couplets. I shall read more to you as the great work progresses. I'm working on a couplet about Lord Cardigan's charge at Balaclava: it's only rough, of course, but it will go, very

54

movingly, rather like this:

> When 'cross the valley dashed the Light Brigade
> Not often had a faster charge been made.'

Roy and I agreed later that we preferred Tennyson.

December 11th

Roy Dracula is thoroughly helpful to me. My Eton and Balliol connections of course give me the entrée to great houses and good families, but he knows a great many people who are not of aristocratic lineage and yet are certainly interesting. Roy's branch of the family, the Ostrava cousins as Uncle Vlad calls them, were always well thought-of. I believe there was some surprise when he married Shirley as her – very minor – part of the family was thought to be seedy: South American connections were even rumoured.

Roy introduced me to their doctor, of whom he had spoken at our first meeting, an agreeable man with rooms in Harley Street and a delightful old house in a Bloomsbury square. Dr Jekyll (remarkably well qualified, I noticed, MD, DCL, LLD, FRS) gave me a routine physical check and reported my health as unusually good. He clicked his tongue a little when examining my teeth and asked a dental colleague, a Mr Wilfred, to examine them. The latter said, in a rather puzzled voice: 'The Count appears to have some proclination of the maxillary canines on a skeletal-two base with chronic marginal gingivitis with calculus. He could at some stage sustain a coronal fracture of the canine exposing dentine which might require a full-veneer crown.'

December 13th

I visited Dr Jekyll's house early this evening. After some interesting discussion in which he developed his belief in the thorough and primitive duality of man we strolled to his laboratory door, which he unlocked. We had each a glass of seltzer and hock, and these we laid down as he explained to me something of the purpose and content of the glazed cabinets filled with chemicals. Then an extraordinary thing happened.

Jekyll had laid down his glass near a beaker on the table: it was filled with a still, pale green liquid from which all ebullition had subsided. Discoursing with some energy – he has a most vivacious way with him – he inadvertedly raised and drained the wrong glass.

The effect was beyond belief. My friend's whole body began to shake and rack, his face to swell and blacken.

'Your butler Poole shall summon a doctor instantly,' I cried, moving to the door, but by the most urgent mouthing and gestures Jekyll made it plain that I should do nothing. As soon as his awful spasms diminished, he lurched to the door and locked it with a savage gesture. Then he spoke in an odd hoarse voice, turning to face me fully as he did so.

But it was not my elegant friend Jekyll who now confronted me: it was a different man, younger, shorter, ugly and misshapen, and above all exuding the most powerful stench of evil I have ever encountered. 'That was an unfortunate mistake,' he mumbled, 'which I shall now rectify.'

With surprising speed he began to mix chemicals in a graduating glass, measuring the minims, adding powders and salts until the whole boiled and smoked in the glass. As the ferment died he drank the mixture, and fell again into the same dreadful convulsions. I watched spellbound. I watched especially the corded hairy hand which moved convulsively towards a thick cane, of a rare, tough and heavy wood. I have no doubts that this evil monster which had replaced my friend Jekyll felt a dark urge to seize it and attack me murderously.

And then, after a long minute or so, the re-transformation was complete, and, pale yet composed, Jekyll stood before me again.

'Cucumber sandwiches,' he said. 'Let us share a large plate of cucumber sandwiches.'

I agreed, and we sat silently until Poole had brought them and departed.

'Glad if you won't mention this,' said Jekyll. 'I haven't told anyone I can do it: did tell poor old Hastie Lanyon, but he upped and died.'

'Do just what?' I demanded, feeling that I deserved a full explanation as well as cucumber sandwiches.

'What you've seen. I can stay as I am, good chap and well respected if a bit boring, or I can turn myself into another chap. I call him Hyde and he's more concerned with the – well, you know, with the lusts of the flesh.'

'How do you make your transformation?'

'Yes. Must have startled you. Don't suppose you can imagine a man transforming himself into something else.'

I said nothing.

'First, there's this potion of mine. Took me a long time to perfect, and even now I'm not too sure about the particular salt which brings on the second colour change. But lately I find increasingly that I'm changing without the potion, always from Jekyll into Hyde. I get forewarning with an indescribable sensation – time to end an interview or a chat – and then in a few minutes I'm raging and freezing with Hyde's passions.'

He paused and said suddenly, 'Oops, here we go again.'

It was not long before the dreadful transformation was yet again complete. Again I watched the brutal furred hand closing on the heavy cane, and I determined to move first. In a few moments there was a strange tableau in the locked laboratory: glowering at each other were an evil potential murderer and a large grey wolf. I stared unwinkingly at him with amber eyes and growled deep behind the ruff of my chest fur: Hyde let fall his great stick.

When Jekyll was again restored to his form – and I with him – he said, 'That's the third dose within one hour. What with that and the cucumber, I get very relaxed bowel motions.'

I expressed my sympathy. Then we regarded each other for some time, ignoring the sandwiches. Both realised that we had, however unavoidably, exchanged knowledge more intimate than was usual between gentlemen.

'Now,' said Dr Jekyll, 'each of us knows the other's extraordinary secret. Must say you nearly frightened the life out of Hyde … Don't suppose you'll tell me how you do it?'

After a silence: 'No, my dear Dracula, I thought not. But can we both then swear never to tell each other's fearful secret to another human being?'

I took his hand – once again a cultured and elegant hand – and wrung it. 'I swear absolutely never to tell another living soul.'

December 14th

I rose early and hastened to Roy Dracula's house to tell him about Jekyll since Roy, by his nature, is certainly outside the terms of my oath not to divulge anything to a 'living soul'.

He was both fascinated and concerned. 'Really,' he said – he was decidedly less urbane than usual – 'I don't know what English public life is coming to if one can't rely on professional men. Gracious me – suppose he had one of these – these turns while he was writing my prescription for gout! I may even have been taking the wrong nostrums.'

I agreed with him. Having seen Mr Hyde, I had no doubt that he would, with pleasure, prescribe arsenic in quantities.

'We must,' said Roy decisively, 'we must both find another doctor. The man who springs immediately to mind is John Watson. He is a thoroughly sound doctor, unlikely to metamorphose into anything, and is generally to be found with an eccentric detective friend of his at 221b Baker Street. Let us lunch early, and call on him this afternoon.'

After lunch a hansom cab set us down at 221b Baker Street and drove off sharply, the wheels showering us with small debris. After some delay a housekeeper, wearing what appeared to be a mob cap, opened the door and ushered us in. Before we had done more than take a few paces into the room or address ourselves to Dr Watson – although I had thanked the housekeeper for escorting us – the doctor's friend, evidently Mr Holmes the detective, spoke peremptorily.

'Don't tell me about them, my dear Watson. Mr Roy Dracula I think I know, but his companion ...'

We all looked at the detective; I think I heard the doctor give a resigned sigh.

'From your voice and appearance, sir, you are a Scot: that dark, Celtic look, that over-perfect English speech. Evidently strong and healthy, probably of a careful medical family. So you'll be a Scots medical student, much concerned with your college games, unless I'm mistaken, since you limp from some sporting injury. Am I not right, sir?'

'Close,' said I. 'Quite close. In fact, I'm Count Dracula from Transylvania, and I'm limping because I've got a stone in my shoe.'

Holmes looked slightly disconcerted. 'Transylvania, eh. Then doubtless you've read my monograph on *Certain Lepidoptera in Transylvania*?'

I regretted that I hadn't, Dr Watson said surely it was the Transvaal not Transylvania, and Mr Holmes gathered his pipe, tobacco and hypodermic syringe and went huffily off to his bedroom. He returned in a few moments, followed by a rumpled housekeeper. 'Mr Holmes,' she was saying crossly, 'I've been wanting to clear the dust and those dreadful things from under your bed for weeks and weeks. Please don't stop me when I'm in the midst of it.'

The detective surveyed me glacially and said, 'Count Dracula, it has given me the greatest pleasure to meet you. I'm going for a walk'; and he left the room.

Dr Watson sounded delighted that we were to be his patients, and we chatted agreeably enough about some of the criminal cases in which he has been involved – his high opinion of Inspector Lestrade of Scotland Yard was evident – but after a while he said anxiously, 'I'm afraid you must excuse me. Must go and see what Holmes is up to. He gets into such difficulties if I'm not about, you know.'

January 12th

Tomorrow I return for my final term at Oxford, which I shall quit with little regret. I see it as a valuable part of my apprenticeship, for the quality of the teaching has been very high, even from married tutors – marriage reputedly makes them totally unconscientious. And I have of course made a limited number of wealthy and agreeable friends.

But I have encountered an atmosphere there almost of frenzy. I recall that at our first meeting my Moral Tutor, perhaps not realising who I was, nor the extent of my resources, advised me to pay my tradesmen termly, since 'should you allow your accounts to run on for a year or two, they mount quite alarmingly'. Then he reminded me that 'you can dress respectably and as a gentleman for £20 a year; College clubs are bound to cost you £3 a year, and – as a resident out of College – your £5 caution money is returnable when you go down.'

Nor have I relished Oxford's obsession with rowing: I have seldom known or cared to know the answer to the frequent question, 'How high is Balliol on the river?' Cricket I have passionately enjoyed; I have hunted with the Heythrop, bathed in the Lasher at Sandford, played some croquet and much whist. But, despite the relief and pleasures of the vacations, it has essentially been a world of academic work, a closed world, and one which I shall leave with some gladness.

June 12th

Another momentous day that could change my life.

After breakfast, Biro, who had already cleared up my private rooms in St Giles, was packing up my effects in my college rooms on Staircase XVIII when I was summoned to the Master's Lodging. Apart from the termly ordeal of handshaking – which I had found less daunting than most – I had not seen a great deal of Dr Jowett. I was a little surprised then at the summons; quite astonished to find Mr Drummond already with him.

The Master asked me to close the door carefully, and began directly.

'My dear Dracula, I am sad that your days here are now over. You have proved an admirable Balliol man. I know that your Schools results will be good: I'm sure you will feel the satisfaction of achieving a First Class in Greats. You have not been an oarsman, but you are a fine cricketer. Your social life has been exemplary: you know and are highly regarded by a wide range of excellently connected people. I recall,' his voice took on a tone of some reverence, 'even sending you with an introduction to Miss Florence Nightingale.' I recollected this as a notably unsocial, indeed daunting, experience, but forbore to comment.

'You seem,' Jowett continued, 'to have the greatest affection for the country you have adopted – more than temporarily, I hope. In some ways you are more English than the English.'

I blushed a little at this praise, and Mr Drummond looked extremely pleased.

'It had been my intention,' Jowett continued, 'this day to be in touch with the Foreign Secretary to ask him to offer you some employment in the service of this country; employment commensurate with your social ease, intelligence and gift for languages. But I now learn from Mr Drummond that my intentions have been anticipated.'

It was not until some hours later, with my farewells made and my tipping completed, that Mr Drummond enlightened my burning curiosity as we sat alone in a first-class GWR compartment en route to London.

'Now, Dracula,' he said, 'let us be plain. James Stock and I are both agents of Her Majesty's Government. We have long hoped that you would ultimately join us in our work.'

'Agents,' I gasped. 'You mean – spies?'

'We prefer the term agents. The work is exciting and dangerous. It demands great loyalty to England. It is mostly conducted abroad – yours would be in Eastern Europe. It is of course well paid, although that is irrelevant to an aristocrat of your wealth. Will you, my dear boy, consider joining us?'

For some seconds we sat in silence, save for the staccato rhythm of the carriage wheels. Then:

'I will,' I cried, clasping his hand.

'In that case,' he said, smiling broadly, 'we will this evening keep an appointment with Kay.'

'Who is she?' I asked puzzled.

'No, no. It is our Chief, once a general. Since he received his KCB he's been known as K.'

As we neared Paddington he asked if I had been keeping up with my Codes and Ciphers, and I assured him that I had.

'And have you been eating paper? You must be ready to destroy Secret Instructions.'

'Regularly. I find that the *Morning Post* gives me some indigestion, but *The Times* is perfectly palatable.'

He seemed relieved.

K had a discreet little house in Goodwin's Court, close to New Row and Covent Garden. He was a stocky man with piercing eyes, and apparently deaf.

'Glad you're joining us,' he bellowed. 'I'll give you the details of your first assignment straight away. Remember, none of this must go beyond these four walls.'

I heard several passers-by outside in the Court stop to listen; K continued in his parade-ground roar.

'Warn you straight away, you'll have one particular enemy. He works for Them, man called Van Helsing; sort of Dutch mercenary. Don't like Dutch fellers:

In matters of commerce the fault of the Dutch
Is giving too little and asking too much
So we'll clap on Dutch bottoms at twenty per cent, twenty per
cent.

Talking of which, do you have the Nameless Vice?'

He swung round on Mr Drummond, and on James Stock who
had just arrived in a flying chaise, and enquired again at the top
of his voice, 'Does he have the Nameless Vice, eh?'

The number of listeners in the Court outside increased
appreciably, and I said nervously, 'Could you explain what the
Nameless Vice is, please?'

The others laughed.

'No problems, no blackmail problems there,' K roared, and I
heard some footsteps go away: they sounded disappointed.
Drummond nodded to James, who went and turned on the taps
in the adjoining bathroom, but the effect hardly diminished K's
volume.

'Have a cough sweet,' said K – I took a square black slab
which looked disgusting but tasted delicious. 'Get a lot of sore
throats myself; can't think why,' he added in a confidential
bellow. 'Now – take notes if you like but you must later
memorise and destroy them – here are your Secret Instructions.'

'You know about the Treaty of San Stefano, Congress of
Berlin, and all that. Since then we back the Austrians against the
Russkis: don't want some great gloomy Slav state pushing right
up to Salonika. We got Herzegovina, Bosnia, the Sandjak for the
Austrians, and we back 'em. Their Graf Andrassy may be shifty,
but anything's better than those awful Russians. Gortchakov,' he
muttered, seemingly looking for a cuspidor. 'Gortchakov.'

'Messy region out there,' K continued. 'All have outlandish
names. Come to think of it, Dracula's a bit odd: think we'll call
you 67.'

I wondered why.

'Got some sound '67 port. Where was I? Yes, funny names; Koloman Tisza, Prince President of Hungary, I ask you. Or Bozo Petrovic — what sort of name is that? Bozo indeed.'

K looked dispirited, but he rallied and shouted at James, 'Get a bottle of port. The '69 from the drawer marked East Europe Confidential. Empty it into four large glasses and we'll get back to business.'

He drank most of his glass in a sort of inhalation, and went on: 'That's the trouble. Outlandish lingo. My fellers can't get round it. There was Louis. Tree, garrotted in Buda-Pesth; David Whiterood, garrotted in Bucharut; Toby Tunnel, disembowelled in Belgrade; Tommy Mountjoy — old Wykehamist, too — stake through his heart in Bratislava. Oh, sorry Dracula,' he added, 'of course I remember about your father being staked. Very sad. Poor show.

'Anyway, Dracula, you won't get picked off like the others. They all went to Angst, that's a town in a bit of Bessarabia the Russkis made the Romanians give way.'

'I know Angst,' I said.

'Good, good. Now there was a Russian spymaster living there in the Hotel Bortello. But he's moved from there — want you to find out where he is now and kill him.'

I swallowed and looked at Mr Drummond and Stock, who both nodded approvingly.

'Kill him with this blowpipe,' said K in a confidential bawl. 'Feller called Bogdanadov. Nasty feller. Show you how to kill him. James, bring in that cat.'

Stock returned with another bottle of port and a large black tomcat with serrated ears. He put the animal on a table some six feet from K: it sat there regarding us balefully, and then began to lap the lees from a port glass. K removed a dart from a small velvet-lined case, fitted it to the blowpipe and blew. The cat, the dart in its fur, shot out of the door.

'Curare-derived,' said K. 'Be dead in two minutes.'

'Why have I got to kill Bogdanadov like that?'

'Simple. It's not an English method. They'll think Johnny

Turk did it. Better they suspect the Turks.'

'Why have I got to kill Bogdanadov at all?'

K furrowed his brow and thought carefully. 'Why are we killing the feller? Refresh me, Drummond.'

Mr Drummond removed his pipe and said quietly, 'Bogdanadov — and Van Helsing and the agents that evil man controls — are paid by the Russians to turn the Herzegovinians against the Austrians. But good Austrian control here is a barrier to the Russians and the growing Slav state that we don't want. So Bogdanadov must be eliminated.'

'Quite well put,' said K, approvingly. 'Well, here's your wallet; money, blowpipe, this month's operating cipher, false moustaches, daguerreotype of Bogdanadov; and the current keyword is "Zilch". Kill him next week if possible, Friday or Saturday are good days, and then return *immediately* and report to me, here personally. Not round about midday, I'm at my Club from 12 to 3.15, and not on Monday or Friday as I spend a little more time at house parties nowadays. And, remember, start back immediately but take a slower route if that's safer. Want to see you again.'

'Where would I find Bogdanov?'

'Shrewd question. We think he's now at the Gradasevic Hotel in Belgrade — you'd call it Beograd, I suppose. Go there, contact our local agent there, Doskos, at a pension called Hristic: he'll tell you everything, make everything easy.'

'Did David and Louis and Toby and Tommy all get advice from Doskos?' I asked rather apprehensively.

'Very shrewd. My word, Drummond, we've got a first-class recruit here. Yes, they did. But Doskos is foreign, you see, doesn't have much English, and my chaps hardly understood a word he said. Louis, David, Tommy and Toby — they'd all be alive today if they'd had the lingo. But,' he was shaking me vigorously by the hand and leading me to the door, 'you'll be all right. You've got the lingo.'

As I slipped out of the door a cross black cat streaked out with me, zig-zagging between the feet of the small crowd outside K's window. I resolved to fortify the poisoned tips of my blow darts. K's great voice followed me as I moved down Goodwin's Court: 'Drummond – James, bring in more port – we've got some serious thinking to do.'

In a few moments I was in the flat in New Row. Erika was there and the ensuing encounter was as delightful and fortifying as ever. But dominant in my mind was intense excitement at my new mission, and a powerful feeling that as long as men like K were at the helm, England and her Empire must grow ever stronger and greater.

June 14th

I write this in the train, for Biro and I have not delayed but are already bound for Beograd. Last night Biro made all the preparations and I told Horrolds I must be breakfasted early since I was going away for a few days. I gave no indication of my destination.

Mrs Merry herself brought in my breakfast. 'Welcome back, sir, welcome back on this beautiful morning. I wish you were remaining longer:

> The flowers are so gay and the grass is so green
> No place in my mind for a thought that is mean.'

'My word, you are a poetess,' I said, smiling.
She turned to me and responded:

> 'If I can write before I die
> One line of purest poetry
> Then none is happier than I
> Not even piggies in their sty.'

Biro, who was preparing to shave me, seemed greatly touched by this.

Before shaving was done a note was delivered by Mr Drummond's man. The bold, if barely decipherable, writing read: 'After all, go first to Hotel Bortello in Angst and blow. Thence Doskos, Belgrade. Thence me. Destroy this. K.'

June 17th

We are in Angst. The regularity of the railway section of our journey is almost monotonous: the punctuality of departures and arrivals; the unfailing willingness of railway staff ....

Most of the inhabitants here seem depressed, although Angst is a pretty town, tumbled up a hillside and pleasantly warm on a dusty Bessarabian evening. My preparations are made, our lodgings secured, the Hotel Bortello reconnoitred (a swarthy gross man exactly corresponding to Bogdanadov's daguerreotype is indeed staying there under the name of Silkinsky), and my blowpipe carefully cleaned to give the maximum muzzle velocity. I shall set off on the critical part of my mission after darkness has come down (and, Biro insists, after I've put down a good supper). If I fail ... this may be the last entry in my Diary. (I find myself strongly regretting that Uncle Vlad was so upset at my dear Father's demise that he never detailed to me what can and cannot kill the Un-Dead.)

June 19th

It was not the last entry, but it came close to that.

I reached the hotel and, Angst being encouragingly free of owls, changed myself into a bat and investigated several windows. Bogdanadov-Silkinsky proved unmistakable; he was in a long, narrow, low-ceilinged attic bedroom with several burly, bearded men of villainous appearance who could have been Kruger's brothers. They were laughing and joking, and I crept through the casement quite unnoticed, folded my wings and tucked myself into a dark corner of the angled ceiling where the light of their single oil lamp would never reveal me.

'And so,' Bogdanadov was saying, with a great guffaw, 'yet another English agent is being sent. Sent to hunt me down in Beograd, while we are all so safe and happy here in Angst.'

'Who is the English agent, and what will be his fate?' asked one prodigiously bearded man.

'This time the agent is not an English milord, but a Transylvanian noble. His name escapes me, but he will not.'

'No?'

'No. Van Helsing will kill him, and painfully. He was experimenting with new types of piano wire when last I saw him.'

As their huge merriment died down, two unfortunate developments arose. Saying, 'And now we must speak in the greatest secrecy', Bogdanadov firmly shut the window; at the same time the hotel cat came in at the door, which one of the men then irritably closed.

Bogdanadov's voice rolled on '... Bosnians will follow me in Herzegovina in agitation and assassination ... the Serbs too ... one day we'll get a Serb to assassinate a royal Austrian archduke, and then the cat will be among the pigeons.'

The hotel cat, unfortunately, was not concerned with pigeons, but with me. It was no larger than K's tom but brindled, rangy and ferocious, and it both detected me and decided to eat me.

At first it stalked along the floor looking hungrily upwards: then it sprang, climbing on to high furniture in the low room and fiercely launching itself at me. Not only did it miss me very narrowly indeed but, worse, it alerted the men. All except Bogdanadov rose to see what was happening.

'Oh look there, it's a bat that it's after.'

'Let's kill it.'

'Knock it down for the cat to eat.'

'I'll get my stick.'

'I'll fetch something from the closet to hit it with.'

This last sentence determined me. 'Not another damned

68

lavatory brush,' I muttered furiously as, with a celerity of which Prince Vlad would surely have been proud, I changed my appearance.

The general reaction to the sudden appearance of a full-grown wolf in the attic room was most satisfactory. The men already standing bolted simultaneously and, although the cat instantly followed through the doorway, it was unable to overtake them as they rushed or fell down the stairs. I had the impression of limbs being broken.

Bogdanadov alone remained. He was still in his chair: I stood between him and the door. We stared at each other. Then I thought that he was the co-murderer of Louis and David, Toby and Tommy – and of me, if chance had fallen differently. My eyes began to glow, the ruff of hair at my neck to rise, I made an involuntary noise deep in my throat.

So did he. He half rose, the rattle of his choking noise intensified, he clutched his chest desperately, and then collapsed to the floor. I sniffed at him quickly and confirmed that his black heart was beating no more. I thought, 'I'm sure they'll blame this on the Turks.'

I changed and fluttered downstairs, past an excited group in the hotel's little vestibule who were divided between scepticism and sending for men with guns. I changed again and strolled home. Biro was waiting with cocoa and Haemozade. Afterwards I climbed into bed saying, 'We leave for Beograd at dawn'; and had an excellent night's repose.

June 21st

We reached Beograd and went straight to the given address of
K's local agent, Doskos. He showed no surprise at seeing us:
indeed he said, 'I had expected you a little earlier.'

He was plump and effusive and sweated much more than I
thought necessary. I mistrusted him instantly. He ushered us into
a small shady courtyard. 'What will you drink, my most
welcome guests? Slivovitz, wine ...'

I had a sudden idea. 'No,' I said. 'In these hot regions I find
ouzo, raki, whatever you call that delicious, cool, colourless
spirit, I find that the ideal drink. My servant here will drink only
water.' I ignored Biro's reproachful eye, and repeated, 'He
drinks only water.'

Doskos engaged in a good deal of shouting and hand clapping,
which enabled me to murmur some quiet words to Biro. Very
soon we were seated at a table with three glasses, two bottles of
ouzo and one pitcher of water.

'Another glass, please,' I demanded imperiously. 'I prefer to
mix the spirit and the water in my mouth.' Ouzo of course
remains colourless until the addition of water, when it takes on a
cloudy appearance: I believe that some lavatory preparations
have similar properties.

We drank our first round; Doskos poured a second, and Biro
and I unobtrusively changed over our glasses.

'So you are another English milord,' said Doskos thoughtfully.

'Yes,' I lied firmly.

'And you do not speak the language of our country? Not at
all?'

'Certainly not.'

'Your servant?'

'It would be agreeable,' I said cuttingly, 'if he could adequately
speak his native English. After that he might conceivably turn to
some foreign tongue.'

70

'You are so brave, so courageous, to venture on dangerous missions in these troubled parts without understanding a word of the language.'

'We English,' I answered loftily, 'have not found it necessary to master languages in order to master the world.'

Doskos beamed at us, poured more ouzo, and shouted to some confederate or crony. When the man came he continued to smile happily at us, showing an expanse of blackened teeth which I always find repellent; but what he actually said, very rapidly in his local tongue, was as follows.

'Go to the Hotel Gradasevic. Tell Van Helsing that another imbecile English aristo is here and will be sent to him for despatch within the half-hour. The aristo will be drunk; he has a servant who will be sober. Both should be killed. And tell him, too, to kill the right man; there was too much trouble when he strangled that visiting Customs Officer by mistake. Tell him this one is wearing an elegant black cloak, velvet, very fine and full and with a scarlet lining; and a black hat, velour, wide-brimmed, which obscures his face. Impress that on him.'

It was almost an hour later that the three of us set off down the street for the Hotel Gradasevic. Biro and I, switching our glasses, had drunk nearly half a bottle each and we walked a little cautiously. Doskos had consumed twice as much and was very intoxicated. As we neared the hotel he kept saying, 'You're a lovely milord. A lovely, dovely, wovely milord.'

'Doskos,' I replied as warmly as I could, 'you are a fine man. I would wish to give you a present. I could see you admiring my hat and my cloak – here, now, take them as gifts.'

Biro and I threw the cape over his shoulders and buttoned it at the neck, its scarlet skirt swirled. We clapped the hat over his eyes, and followed discreetly as he lurched into the hotel. Almost immediately we heard a hoarse grasping cry of deadly finality. I could sense the approving shades of the avenged David and Louis, Toby and Tommy.

Then Biro and I looked at each other. We knew it was time speedily to leave Beograd, for we were two against many, and

71

they were alerted. But where to go? The answer blazed in the eyes of us both.

'We have accomplished much,' I cried. 'Although I must soon return and report to K, we have the time, we have the chance just to see, to see again, our own dear home. All speed then, all speed to our beloved Castle Dracula!'

June 23rd

As we came up towards the pass – both Biro and I urging the calèche driver to greater speed – I recognised the familiar boundaries of the great Dracula estate and my heart rose. Rose only to fall again as I looked at the land and fearful doubts assailed my mind.

For where the sheep had grazed on the higher pastures, I saw no sheep; in the rich valley falling away below, only a few scrawny kine; while in the rolling hectares of cornfields, sweep upon sweep of them, mere traces remained of last year's crop, unharvested, blackened, ruined and worthless.

As we tore up the long drive I could see the sheep pens and cattle byres empty, the pigsties deserted; only the wolves' pen was filled with creatures now obscenely fat, but none the better-tempered for that. We stopped briefly and I saw my old adversary Casanova, who snarled and instinctively wiped his paw across his nose. Then we sped on to the great steps of the Castle: as we mounted them a pathetic figure tottered out from the huge hammered doors.

It was Footescu. Nor was his tottering surprising, for added to his natural senility was the effect of a huge ball and chain round his left ankle.

'Master, Master!' he cried. He threw himself into my arms and in the emotion of the moment the pain of the iron ball on my instep passed unnoticed, although I later lost a toenail. 'Oh, you've come to save me from those evil men,' he sobbed.

'What evil men?'

'Tomas and Niklaus – and the others.'

'Sit down,' I said firmly. 'You may sit in my presence, good Footescu. And before I enter my own castle, tell me what is happening here.'

Biro knelt by his side and in a moment had freed the old man from his encumbrance, using a small ingenious tool – 'It is chiefly for getting stones from horses' hooves,' he said with his quick smile, 'given to me by the servant of an English cornet, a Mr Baden-Powell.' He also gave poor Footescu a draught of slivovitz from his flask and the old man began to talk, feebly at first but soon with animation, his voice soaring and diving, sometimes croaking, sometimes squeaking, giving a yet stranger effect to his extraordinary tale.

'They have a dogma, Master, and they began to act on it the day you left. They want to take the money from the rich lords and masters like you and make the serfs and peasants rich instead.'

Grimly I said, 'They're certainly taken the money from me: are the serfs and peasants —'

'Starving. All starving. No money, no work: it's terrible to see.' He blew his nose on a cloth used for the silver cleaning.

'Immediately they started things called Unions. For the stockmen, the Stockman's Operative Defence Union, SODU; for the under-bailiffs who added up the bushels and checked the weights at the sales, the Doing All the Sums Union, DASU; for the workers in the field, the Union for Gathering Harvest, UGH; and for the women and girls who take out drinks and food in the long working days, the National Association of Refreshment Providers, NARP.'

'Did our peasants want to join these – these organisations?'

'Several refused. They were garrotted.'

'Then who,' I asked ominously, 'who led them?'

'Indeed, Master, it is not what you think,' he said passionately. 'None here at Castle Dracula could or would lead them. The leaders were brought from Russia, Bucktov for SODU, Roddish for DASU, Mossevsky for UGH, Mrs Barbitznin for NARP.

'At first,' he continued, 'all went quite well for them. Money

73

came in – and they spent it: all six took a holiday in Italy where I believe they were drunken all the time.'

'At our Master's expense,' said Biro angrily.

'Indeed. But then trouble began between them. Let me try to recall how it went.' He tapped his aged brow to a hollow echo. 'You will remember how all were paid equally – and very well, when the harvests and the markets were good. But DASU said they were skilled adders-up and should be paid twice anyone else and should have very big pensions, and SODU said they were skilled too and should have two men for each herd or flock, and UGH said they were the largest and therefore the most powerful and must have the same as the others, and NARP said they provided essential services and must have the same and it would be an insult to Womanhood if they didn't.'

'NARP said *that*?' Biro's voice was incredulous.

'Mrs Barbitznin said it very loudly. She has a very shrill voice. Indeed she broke the glass chandelier in the north end of the Great Hall, although I think it was already cracked from when your so-revered Uncle Vladimir hit it with an under-footman in 1832.'

'Continue your story.' I was consumed with impatience.

'Then Tomas and Niklaus doubled *all* their wages.'

'And so they were satisfied?'

'Indeed, no. The situation was just as before: all were still equal, none wished to be equal. They all went on strike.'

Footescu paused in weary recollection, and Biro passed his flask again.

'The strike dragged on. Each was determined to be paid more than the others. They never talked: occasionally they met and screamed terrible words at each other, about money, about demarcation.'

'Demarcation?' I didn't remember this from Eton or Balliol.

'Yes, Master. For example, UGH used to keep a tally of the sheaves as they put them into stooks, but DASU said that must be their adding work and they needed more staff to do it. And over the ploughing, UGH said it was over their fields and for their

74

crops; SODU said it was their oxen that did it.'

I was becoming dazed with these acronyms.

'Then, Master, they appointed the schoolmaster to act as conciliator.'

'That stupid little man with small origins and large words?'

'The same, Master. Simonyi Maculesky. They told him: produce a document which is a model for future fair and objective bargaining, or we'll smash your face in.'

'What did he deliver?'

Footescu fumbled in his deplorable clothing and brought out a dreadfully crumpled piece of paper: 'This is a copy.'

Maculesky's conciliation document read: 'We, DASU, as aforesaid hereinafter being parties of this, the first and subsequent parts, hereafter referred to as parties of the first part, or the first disputants, do either singly, jointly or together, in this solemn and binding agreement resolve in fraternal co-operation with our brothers in SODU hereinafter referred to as the parties of the second part or second disputants. We being as heretobefore the parties of the first and second parts and being thus unavoidably engaged with the first, second, third and fourth disputants do and in this solemn and irreversibly binding agreement hereafter agree to continue fraternal discussions whether jointly, together or separately on an on-going basis and to conduct the same in brotherly co-operation in consideration of the employers granting a consolidated increase of 100 per centum per annum.'

Footescu sighed. 'They all used bad words at little Maculesky for this document, and Tomas and Niklaus applied to double the wages yet again, but it was no good. Anyway,' he added, 'by now it would have cost much more to get in the harvest and rear the stock than could ever be got selling in the market, so nothing could be any good.'

'And now?' I asked, very quietly.

'And now the stock has died, the crops are unharvested and ruined, the peasants starving. Some have gone to other villages: some even to other countries.'

Biro and I looked at each other. 'This,' he said, 'could never happen in England.'

We went into the Castle. Tomas and Niklaus were not there – a footman said they had left a few hours earlier on hired horses – but they had left a note: 'Whilst our theories for the management of labour and the estate economy are absolutely sound, they seem here to have met with some little local difficulties, and we are therefore leaving to put our theories into effect in other countries. We have certainly eliminated the surplus value.'

Four tipsy trade unionists were there, however. I was feeling extremely angry and very strong, and personally put them in the dungeons; Bucktov, Mossevsky and Roddish in one, Mrs Barbitznin in another. Over the sparsest of suppers I reviewed the situation. This was a grave personal misfortune, but nevertheless as an aristocrat, an OE, a Balliol man, my duty was clear. My mission must first be completed; my report made before I could honourably return to Castle Dracula. I told Biro to leave at dawn for Tirgoviste, to give a full account to Uncle Vlad, to ask him to deal with the situation and the prisoners, and to remain under my Uncle's orders until my return.

Then I sent again for Footescu. 'Why did I never learn of all this?' I demanded.

'Master, none of us can write. But – but, I can read a little; I read their letters: had they known that I knew what I knew, I would not merely have been shackled, but strangled.'

I puzzled out this sentence and asked him to explain.

'You have a major-domo in London? His name is Horrolds? He is your enemy, I think because you did not like a lady friend of his. And he has made a friend of another enemy of yours.'

'I have few enemies. Even,' I turned to Biro, 'even Hooley is now a – a chum.'

'This enemy is called Van Helsing.'

'So,' I murmured.

'He persuaded Horrolds that no mail, no letters should reach you from Transylvania. Your friends, your bankers, all who have written to you from our country have written in vain. Horrolds has intercepted the letters.'

76

I gave such money as I had to Footescu, and then an extraordinary thought struck me. 'Biro! I have *no* money, no money at all. This is unimaginable.'

He was a rock at this terrible time. 'Dear Master,' he said firmly, 'a footman will go at first light for the great Prince Vlad. I shall go with you to the port of Varna. I have a little money from my wages – of course all my money is yours – and with that you, as one of the Great Un-Dead, can be shipped safely back to England, consigned to Messrs Carter, Paterson & Co. And I mean safely, Master, for had we the money for the Orient Express, who knows what evil agent of Van Helsing, perhaps equipped with piano wire, might not be on that train.'

I am not a vindictive man, and in any event my Uncle would deal with the miscreants, but I did a cruel thing before leaving for Varna at dawn. I moved Mrs Barbitzin into the same dungeon as the others. Her strident voice was still echoing as I went down the balustraded steps, but I *think* I heard Roddish sigh, 'May my release by impalement be hastened.'

July 6th

I hope this voyage will require few entries. Here I am, safe and comparatively snug in a wooden box filled with my native earth in the hold of the *Demeter*.

July 12th

The evidence of my ears tells me that we have cleared the Bosphorus and the Dardanelles and seen the last of intrusive and highly corrupt Turkish Customs Officers. I now have to make a difficult decision.

As one of the Un-Dead, I can perfectly well put myself in a cataleptic state in the box of my native earth and remain there until we reach Whitby. I wish it was to be a south-coast port rather than Whitby; and I wish it was not the *Demeter*, which is a Russian schooner and excessively dirty and ill-run. But needs must where that devil Van Helsing drives, and Biro has really managed excellently. Yet it seems a terrible waste of two or three weeks. Further, my native earth has evidently been associated with a midden, which is decidedly distasteful. Worse still, garlic heads, much bruised, seem extensively mingled with it. So I think I shall rise every night and wander about the ship: I am anxious to undertake some serious thinking about the metaphysical theories of F.H. Bradley, which were creating such a stir in Oxford when I left — only three weeks ago, although it somehow seems longer.

July 16th

I am increasingly unenthusiastic about this vessel. The Captain, Second Mate, cook and five hands are typical Russians, glum, surly and little cleaner than the Turks. But the First Mate, a Romanian, is far worse: unbalanced and given to furious rages, he should be ranting on a politician's hustings rather than in a sailing schooner's deck house. He hates the Russians — who reciprocate — and last night I saw him stalk up behind one of them called Petrovsky, brain him with a belaying pin, and pitch the corpse overboard. Things like that do *not* happen in the English mercantile marine, and as for the Royal Navy, I have never believed the absurd song and dance they made in the case of William Budd.

August 2nd

Most unsatisfactory voyage. It was extremely rough in the Mediterranean before we passed Gibraltar; even rougher as we beat our way through the Bay of Biscay and round Ushant. Clearly I am not a good sailor, and have the same feelings of nausea on a pitching ship as when I first took flight with Uncle Vlad. The food is atrocious. I spend a good deal of time in the cookhouse, but whilst there is plenty of available food, it's mostly too nasty to eat.

At one point, in the Straits, we passed close to a huge east-bound vessel, the P & O's *Kaisar-i-Hind*, reputedly of 4,000 tons and with oil lamps rather than the usual candles in the smoking room. She was spotless and brilliantly painted; the passengers waved cheerfully over the rails at us. The *Kaisar-i-Hind*'s Master addressed us over his loudhailer pointing out, courteously yet firmly, that the *Demeter* was a great deal closer than she had any right to be. Our Captain replied with a torrent of obscenity and blasphemy, but as he delivered this with a broad grinning face and in a North Russian dialect, the *Kaisar-i-Hind* evidently took it as an apology.

Our Captain, who incidentally is called Kitsov, comes from one of those Finnish-originated tribes in the extreme north of the country, and speaks his own tongue with so thick and incomprehensible an accent that the rest of his awful crew frequently misunderstand him.

Bell-Mountain, usually shrewd in such matters, believes that one day people will actually go on ship's cruises, in the Mediterranean, for pleasure. Looking at the *Kaisar-i-Hind* this seems just possible: looking at the *Demeter* it does not.

The present plenitude, against the early scantness, of our ship's food is of course because of the First Mate's continuing madness.

So far he has killed the cook and the Second Mate and four of the hands. (Can he have been influenced by W.S. Gilbert's recent and amusing ballad, *The Yarn of the Nancy Bell*?) Only the Captain and one of the crew remain, and, despite his high Slavonic density, I would have thought the Captain must realise that his Mate is a madman who has got rid of the men one by one.

I feel I should volunteer to help this remaining pair to work the ship. But what use could I be? It might have been different had I been a wet bob.

August 3rd

A frightening moment. I was in the cookhouse rather dispiritedly going through the great quantities of food. The weather was calm enough — we must be in the North Sea by now — but the *Demeter* heeled sharply over from an unexpected breeze, and I lost my footing and tumbled into a large open tub. Suddenly, as I was extricating myself with some difficulty, I looked up and saw the Mate framed in the doorway.

He had a fearfully long knife in his hand which he kept driving savagely into space, and as I was fairly certain that he had killed the last of the hands on the previous night, I expected a sudden maniacal attack.

It did not come. He stared at me, eyes rolling and face convulsed with fear. Then, inexplicably, he howled, 'Save me. Save me!', rushed to the rail, shouted to the bemused Captain at the wheel, 'The sea will save me from him, and it is all that is left'; and leaped overboard.

I subsequently realised that the barrel into which I'd fallen was of flour so that my black suit and dark hair were overlaid with a curious whiteness. Even so, I wouldn't have thought that my appearance had anything to do with the mad Mate's suicide.

August 9th

A very unsettling day. Thoroughly fed up with this interminable voyage, I had for several days retired into a catalepsy in my smelly soil. Judge of my amazement when, clambering out for a breath of fresh air, I discovered the *Demeter* running through the night with all sails set before a most appalling wind which roared like thunder. The Captain, an expression of intense concentration on his bovine face, was seated at the wheel – indeed, I observed, had even lashed his hands to the wheel – and was gazing fixedly at the rapidly approaching entrance to the harbour, a harbour vividly lit by searchlights: Whitby harbour, I hoped.

Obviously he needed some help. I thought that if perhaps I steered, he could lower the sails so that, should the ship escape the fury of the wind and enter the harbour, it would not be dashed to destruction on a pier.

'Er, excuse me,' I said to the Captain.

He did not reply, but continued to mutter to himself, a complicated mixture of prayer and obscenity. I cleared my throat. 'Er – hum. Humph.' He looked fixedly ahead, so I said quite loudly, 'Hello, sailor.'

This proved all too effective. He started uncontrollably and leaped to his feet – only to be brought down again by his self-lashed wrists – staring at me in wild and utter amazement. I'm ashamed to say I had not made a proper toilet since falling into the flour barrel, and I was about to apologise for my unusual appearance when he suddenly let out a dreadful shriek: 'I shall save my soul and my honour as a captain.'

After which he went through very much the same performance as the late Bogdanadov had so recently done, and I was left feeling thoroughly aggrieved that a well-meant offer of help had been answered by a fatal heart attack.

My own position was unenviable. The ship, now steered by a dead man, passed through the entrance to the harbour and was driving at breakneck speed at an ugly-looking pier jutting out under the east cliff. I supposed I was shortly to be dashed to death. To transform myself into a bat would be no solution, with the raging storm and sea-spray. Sighing, I went below, recovered my Diary and placed it between my teeth. Then I changed into a wolf and leaped into the furious waters just before the schooner struck. I engaged in a powerful dog paddle; some of the spectators on shore cheered me on (probably SPCA members) and I soon felt the shingle between my paws.

I did not delay to view the wrecked ship or the Captain's corpse — Whitby citizens were rushing to do that — but made all haste to find a quiet place for rest and reflection, for, seawards, the dawn was now lightening the sky. To my irritation, as I lolloped past the Tate Hill Pier Coal and Coke Merchants a large, foul-mouthed dog, mostly mastiff, shot through a gap in the fence and attacked me ferociously. He was as clumsy as he was vicious so I killed him quickly, and trotted on feeling distinctly shaken.

Then I had a piece of good fortune. A large residence lay before me, its owners on holiday (in England it seems to be perfectly safe to leave one's home obviously empty), and by the conservatory a small snug ark-like construction. Gilt lettering announced 'Home, Sweet Home — for Fido'; it was warm, the absent Fido's blanket was clean and snug, and I fell into a much-needed sleep.

August 10th

My fortune is changing. When I awoke I returned to my normal form and, sitting on a garden seat just by the gateway of the empty house, tried to improve my clothes and my appearance. After what I had been through this was not easy, but I must have had some success, for a voice suddenly called to me. 'Count Dracula?'

Looking up in utter astonishment I recognised Mrs Mina Harker, the typewriter who had married – foolishly in my view – the solicitor's clerk, Jonathan Harker. There she was, a decidedly pretty girl and bold as brass – I remembered how cheekily she had winked at me when she came with Harker to my Piccadilly house.

'What on earth are you doing here?' I demanded.

'That's easy,' she said, 'staying with my dear friend Lucy Westenra in Chatham Street. It's healthy here, if a bit boring. But, more to the point, what, heavens to Betsy, are *you* doing here? And looking so – well, so disreputable?'

I told her, more or less truthfully, that I had come from the wrecked *Demeter*, that for reasons of Transylvanian state this must remain secret, and that I had lost all my baggage and money.

'Gosh,' she said, 'how exciting.'

She looked excited. She also, I began to notice, looked like Erika in a certain mood.

'Look here, Count,' she continued, and I was grateful to find her so decisive, 'you stay here. This is the Boycotts' house – they're an incredibly rich Yorkshire family and they're on holiday in Switzerland now – and Mrs Westenra's holding their keys. I'll be back soon, and I'll bring some money to get you to London.'

'That's wonderful.' I felt my gratitude growing.

'Now,' she sat down very close to me, 'my mean-minded husband would undoubtedly charge you interest on the loan, I shan't, but I want you in return to come back to Whitby and spend a few days here with me? Done?'

'It's healthy here,' I replied instantly. 'Done.'

It seemed no time at all before we were in the house and while she cooked breakfast – underdone liver, kidneys and gammon – I was in Sir Ray Boycott's bathroom, which was quite grand and *en suite* with his bedroom, washing, shaving, cleaning my teeth and generally feeling a great deal better. After breakfast she pointed to an iron which she was heating.

'Right, Count, go up to the bedroom and take your clothes off.'

'I beg your pardon?'

'I'm not going to iron and press your clothes while you're still wearing them.'

She did press them, surprisingly well, but it was some time later. She proved as happily energetic as Erika, and I doubted if Sir Ray's bed had seen so much activity for years. And when, from affection and sheer necessity. I bit her very lovingly in the neck, she responded by happily nibbling by ears. As we lay quietly afterwards, our flanks touching, I said, 'I'm certainly not complaining, but what made you decide on this – this course of action?'

She giggled. The fact that she is a thoroughly common girl does not make her giggle any less attractive. 'Several things. I yearned for you like anything when first I saw you. And Jonathan is such a frightful bore. And I know you're not a saint, because he told me about Erika's little flat … she's not always there, though?' she asked sharply.

'No.'

'And then Lucy Westenra here is a dear friend, of course, but she really does queen it around with all these people proposing to her, and the grand marriage she is going to make.'

'Who are the suitors?'

'Well, assorted curates come to supper, some have adenoids, some acne, some both. When they've proposed to her and she's rejected them, they turn to me. And they're so dreary that they make even my Jonathan seem like, well, fun.' She wriggled agreeably.

'Then there's a terrible gloomy Dr Seward who runs a huge lunatic asylum near London and only talks about one patient, chap who eats spiders.' She gave a shiver: 'Fancy eating spiders. Not baked or grilled or anything, but alive. Ugh!'

I shivered, too, for in the back blocks of my memory there stirred some fearful story that Uncle Vlad had told me about his time in Turkish captivity. We clung together involuntarily.

'The dismal doctor proposed to Lucy and was turned down. Same fate befell a brash boy from Texas, Quincey Morris. A whirl with him might have been just bearable, but he turned out to be a chum of the chap she really is going to marry.'

'Anyone I know?' I thought it unlikely.

'Quite likely, Dracula darling. He's the Hon. Arthur Holmwood. But one of Jonathan's better-class clients told him that the Hon. Arthur got dropped from London society a year or two ago over some gambling scandal.'

'I know. I was there.'

'Ooh, Dracula,' she said. 'You *are* grand!'

She giggled and went on. 'Just the same it'll be a great step up for Lucy. I mean, she'll be a *Lady*.'

'You're certainly not meeting very thrilling people.'

'No. There's a great big Irishman who's all right. Called Bram Stoker: writes awful books and is in with the theatricals, I think. And the Hon. Arthur brought a friend last time whom I *didn't* like ever so much. Foreign. Can't remember his name.'

I nodded drowsily.

'Yes, I can,' she said suddenly. She rummaged in her handbag on the bedside table and produced a pasteboard card. It read: 'Abraham Van Helsing, MD, DPh, DLitt.'

I rose from the bed like a rocketing pheasant. 'When, my dearest Mina,' I demanded, 'is the next connection to London?'

A full evening. From King's Cross I went urgently by hansom to Goodwin's Court, and there reported to K.

'Getting a bit worried about you,' he said.

I explained about my shortness of cash and the length of my voyage.

'Yes,' he continued, 'I'd already heard about Bogdanadov meeting his end. Stock was in Vienna and got wind of it. Now just how did it happen?'

Bearing in mind Mr Drummond's repeated injunction that 'an English gentleman will tell the truth and shame the Devil', I kept as closely to the facts as possible.

'Bogdanadov's fellow-conspirators left the room. So I emerged and fixed him with my accusing eyes — '

'Fat lot of good that would do — '

— 'and I snarled at him — '

'What did you snarl?'

'Er, "I am here to end your murderous and evil career".'

K sniffed. 'And that gave him a heart attack?' He then brightened. 'Of course, his constitution may already have been weakened. Mine is, you know. Very often I drink a bottle or so of port and I get a severe pain just here – ' his large, strong, well-manicured hand covered several intercostal spaces ' – so I suppose a slight shock might finish me any day. Like Bogdanadov.'

He gave himself a large glass of port, and me a small one.

'And Doskos, eh. Double agent, was he? Remember saying to Livingstone-Tachbrook – very nice Old Harrovian – when he appointed Doskos, "Trotty," I said – he was always known as "Trotty" – "Trotty, you trusts such Greeks/As English speaks/Seldom and circumspectly." Didn't take my warning. Murdered in Macedonia two years later: thicker piano wire than usual.'

K blew his nose and drank his port. 'Poor old Trotty. So I had doubts about Doskos. But you've done very well. It's what I said, of course, it's knowing the lingo that does it.'

He looked at his watch, and went on briskly. 'Two things now. Back to Whitby and Van Helsing. He's their chief European agent: friends in high places, accessories in the gutters. We call him The Jackal. In a crisis, of course, you're licensed to kill him. Secondly, money: sorry about your financial problems.'

'They are only temporary,' I said. 'My Uncle, the Prince Vlad, will see that work is resumed on our estates, which are vast and rich. He will dissolve the trade unions and impale their leaders, so there is no reason why all should not soon be happy and prosperous again.'

'Meanwhile?'

'Meanwhile I shall let off my large Piccadilly property. And I have a small flat near here — '

'I know.' K eyed me shrewdly.

'And I shall let that, too. It will be a fresh experience for a Dracula, a Szekely, to have to devise means of saving income. But I shall do it.'

He thanked me again, warmly. He thanked me, more practically, with a useful bag of sovereigns. Then, adding that the current password was Gooch, he bade me farewell. He had not raised his voice during the entire interview, so I feared that he must have had an extremely sore throat.

Next to Jonathan Harker. As he is now in charge of the London office of the West Country solicitors who originally employed him (injudiciously in my opinion) to come to Castle Dracula, he now lives in quite a neat little house in Bloomsbury. It was some time before he responded to my knockings on his door: when he took me up, rather breathlessly, to his drawing room I noticed two half-drunk glasses of wine and a smell of inferior perfume. I realised that the readiness of Mina's infidelity was due to more than the strength of the Whitby air.

I crisply explained that he was immediately to rent my two London properties, but only on short leases as my fortunes would soon be restored, and that he was to act as my rent collector. I declined a glass of wine — my taste in wines, naturally good, has been much improved by a series of vinous dinners with Cousin Roy, dinners which Shirley Dracula fortunately does not attend as she has trouble with her legs, and I would find it hard to stomach the vinegary and unclassified stuff that Harker offered.

'Is Mrs Harker at home?' I enquired.

'Alas, no. She is staying with her friend Lucy Westenra up in Whitby. They are the dearest of friends, and Lucy is shortly to marry into the Peerage.'

'You must miss her greatly.'

'Indeed, yes. In her absence I generally bring work back from our offices, and spend the evenings conveyancing.'

As I rose to leave there seemed to be a suppressed noise from the adjoining bedroom.

When I reached the small residence in New Row, Erika was there. She has a heart as large as her physique, for when I told her fully of my temporary difficulties, she instantly said: 'Poor darling Dracula. How very fortunate that my godmother, a loud-voiced woman who bred dogs called Woodcott, died and left me a little legacy. It's of 250 guineas and I insist on lending it to you.'

'And I insist that when I repay, it shall be at very substantial interest.'

'You can start paying some interest now,' she replied, enfolding me in her powerful and affectionate arms.

August 12th

I rose very early this morning, filled with energy, and hastened to Half Moon Street. Mr Drummond was still in his bath – his enthusiasm for his daily cold tub remains undiminished – but who should greet me at the door but my dear Biro. Our happy reunions made, he said: 'Dear Master, if I have disobeyed your orders in coming back, it is because the Prince Vlad bade me return to your side.'

'I am more than delighted to see you. But tell me all that passed at the Castle while I was on that damned *Demeter*.'

'It is better than we had feared. The union leaders were killed. The men made a great deal of unnecessary noise; the woman was brave, although she kept crying, "Rights for Women!" and "Burn your *soutien-gorge!*". Your revered Uncle, the Prince, presided over the ceremony. He has such a sense of style and taste.'

I agreed, although when Biro showed me his drawings of the executions – he really has a great gift – I didn't feel too enthusiastic.

He continued his tale: 'Then we found that one locked granary, recorded as being empty, was full of grain.'

'A bad clerical error.'

'I think not. Bucktov said it was an arrangement, like when in Russia things fall off the back of a droshky. They would have profited from it. And then we have replenished our stock of cattle and sheep, especially sheep.'

'How did we pay for that?'

'We didn't. They are bought on interest-free credit. The merchants weren't keen at first, but when Prince Vlad said he thought it an excellent idea and did they disagree with him? – Well, they became quite enthusiastic.'

He hastened on. 'Dear old Footescu sends you his deepest respects. He's very wandering, now, and his hair gets in his eyes, but he is a brave and loyal old man.'

'I know. I know.'

'And the new chief bailiff is very amiable. He's particularly good on sheep; indeed he looks and sounds like a sheep. He's called Arapad Howkoja, and he's a wonderfully hard worker.'

I began to feel greatly encouraged.

'And I should also tell you, Master, that Mr Drummond knows of your temporary plight, and will ask you to make your home here and accept a temporary allowance. I heard him talking to Mr Stock about it. Mr Drummond said, "I must give him an allowance, but Count Dracula is such a very proud man – how d'you think he'll take it?" – "Why monthly, of course," said Mr Stock and they laughed merrily.'

I had to turn my head away, so overcome was I at the ready kindness of my good English friends.

'But, Master,' Biro concluded a little sadly, 'it does distress me to see your wonderful Castle, our great home, so empty and bare now. All those great rooms, that should be filled with life and people, now deserted.'

After a moment: 'Biro, a thought has struck me. In a week or so, when we have completed other pressing business, remind me of this conversation. And now, please go to my tailor, whose bill I fortunately paid last year, and obtain a scarlet-lined cloak and black hat identical to those we sacrificed in Beograd.'

My meeting with Mr Drummond was moving. He congratulated me warmly on my successful mission, and then with a touching mixture of kindness and embarrassment made me the offer of an allowance. His face was lit with relief when I accepted.

'And now,' I told him, 'for 347 Piccadilly.'

I had hoped first to meet the horrible Horrolds. Alas, it was Mrs Merry and her daughter whom we first encountered, coming briskly and happily down the balustraded staircase. I told Biro to break the news to the daughter – I was so concentrating on my forthcoming interviews that I failed to notice that he chose to do this in the servants' sleeping quarters – while I told her mother of my plans.

As soon as she realised that her employment with me was, for the time being at least, to be ended, Mrs Merry fell into a terrible state:

'The sun is shining brightly to say good day to you
And now you bring such awful news I must go boo-hoo-hoo.'

And suiting the action to her words she burst into plangent tears.

In vain I tried to comfort her – 'Excellent references ... probably for only a few months ... three months' pay in lieu of notice ... ' – nothing stilled her noisy distress. She sobbed wildly:

'I should like to dig a deep dark hole
And lie down in it as if in my bed
As if I were a furry wee mole
Or a titmouse after being fed.'

Telling her to be in touch with me in Half Moon Street when she was recovered, I hastened on to confront Horrolds. I found him in his pantry, smoking a pipe and drinking my brandy. He had with him an intensely fat man, who looked both Middle European and scoundrelly. I said very quietly and without more ado, 'Horrolds, you will leave my service today. You will remove your effects immediately. You will receive no further pay from me, nor will I give you a reference.'

As he started up, I added grimly, 'You well know the reasons why.'

After a pause – 'Georgie, please go,' he told his obese friend, who reluctantly went – he replied, in a coaxing way which I found quite odious, 'Come now, sir, I've had my troubles – been blown off-course – but can't we sit round the table, have beer and sandwiches, discuss the matter, reach a reasonable compromise?'

'Even you can't drink beer on top of my Napoleon brandy,' I said crossly. 'You intercepted my letters. You were an ally of my

91

enemies. You will depart from this house now, and never return.'

Leaving Biro to tell the other servants, I strode straight out into Piccadilly. As I did so, I saw Harker going in with a lady, evidently a possible tenant. I instantly noticed (so greatly does the human in me dominate the Un-Dead) that the lady had ample *maquillage* and excessive *décolletage*.

August 13th

With my business in London done, I am quite pleased to be back in Whitby where the Royal Hotel, though modest, is comfortable and the air, as at the adjoining town of Scarborough, invigorating. After my sufferings on the schooner – I shall never again accept that sea voyages are good for the health – I need invigorating. Further, although I have repaid Mina her loan (suppressing a guilty thought that I am robbing Erika to pay Mina) she is still making considerable demands on me; demands which it is both a duty and a pleasure to fulfil.

Mina has introduced me to her friends, the Westenras, who have taken a house here for their holiday. Mrs Westenra is harmless and agreeable; Lucy is pretty and extremely vivacious. I found her quite excruciating. But I cannot write unkindly about her, for her flushed and hectic colour indicates that she is far from well. I have little doubt that the poor girl has a galloping consumption, but Arthur Holmwood (a moist young man) and Dr Seward (whose medical expertise is presumably limited to lunacy) and Quincey Morris (who comes from a small township called Dallas and wears a dreadful snakeskin hat, indoors as well) all insist that there are other causes, highly sinister or pseudo-occult, for her continuing illness. When I learned that she has been discovered wandering barefoot round the local churchyard – a highly exposed spot – I am not surprised at her decline.

Lucy proved very affectionate towards me, kissing me warmly and unnecessarily, to the deadly envy of a pair of curates. But as part of her – seemingly unsuccessful – treatment is a generous employment of garlic, whilst I clean my teeth at least four times daily, I found the encounter distasteful.

Holmwood evidently remembered me well enough from the evening of his humiliation at Cotterell Castle. So too did his friend Van Helsing, who called that evening as we were sitting in the garden. He was drinking hock and seltzer, his wary jackal's eye taking me in, and suddenly I saw his hand start and his drink spill. His gaze was fixed on my black hat and black cape, scarlet-lined.

I leaned forward: 'My cape interests you?'

'A friend of mine,' he answered levelly, 'was wearing just such a cape when he died.'

'How sad. Where was that?'

'In Belgrade. Have you been to Belgrade, Count?'

'We Draculas, we Szekelys, are accustomed to travel a great deal.'

'You may travel further than you expect.' Van Helsing sounded far from agreeable.

August 14th

Staying at the Royal Hotel is the Bram Stoker of whom Mina had spoken, who proves to be a writer of sorts and a business associate of the actor, Henry Irving. At first I thought he should be 'convicted of the awful crime/of being bright at breakfast time' (is Mrs Merry influencing *me* as well?) but he is so genuinely amiable and good-natured that people forgive his fearful jolliness and his massacre of the English language (the Irish seem impervious to the gravity of this murder, as indeed of any other). He seems to know everyone and everything, and had even heard of my temporary embarrassment.

'Wish I could put you in the way of making some money.' This would have been an intolerable impertinence in anyone else, but he so obviously means well that I quite forgave him. I think my English education has made me more tolerant than my dear Father or Uncle Vlad. Cousin Roy seems very mellow, too, even if Cousin Shirley does not.

'You'd make a wonderful illusionist, you know. With your great cloak – real style, real class.'

I bowed and accepted the compliment. We were in his hotel room drinking some whiskey which, he assured me, some Irish friends of his had prepared in their very own still. It made up in power what it lacked in taste.

'You don't have any illusions from your part of the world, d'you, Count? Something romantic and mysterious, from one of the Celebration Mountains? I'd love to go to Transylvania: don't suppose I ever will.'

'What sort of illusions, Stoker?'

'Well … ' he paused. 'Seeming to turn people into goldfish or owls or something like that. An illusion of that kind – well, I know the syndicate which is opening the new Conquest Theatre in Scarborough next Saturday. I could get you 20 guineas a week for something like that.'

'Done,' I said, and we shook hands on it.

August 15th

I awoke this morning feeling an instant need for my tinted glasses, and Biro quickly followed my morning Haemozade with some Carlsbad salts. I told him of my foolish undertaking and warned him of the perils of Mr Stoker's whiskey.

'Can you go back on your word, Master?'

'With the deepest reluctance. But I fear I must.'

Biro pondered for some while. I lay quite still, hoping that I might feel better. Then: 'Sir, I have a plan. Pam Merry and I have so often been to the Music Halls together, and my plan is based on that.'

'Tell me,' I said firmly, and he did.

Before dinner this very evening we gave a trial show in my

room, with Bram Stoker as audience. Biro had bought the familiar coffin in which I had embarked at Varna from a fisherman who had acquired it after the wreck. We stood it upright, I entered, Stoker examined its every side, Biro closed the lid, a minute's pause and he opened it — empty save for a bat. Then the reverse procedure, and I stepped out, cloaked and elegant.

Stoker was astounded. He asked me to do it again, which was tiresome, but I did.

'Amazing, amazing,' he kept saying. 'For the life of me I can't see how it's done. Seen all sorts of tricks and illusions in London, but never anything to beat that.'

'It is,' I assured him, 'a very old Carpathian illusion.'

August 17th

After dinner in our hotel, Bram Stoker proudly produced the contract for my signature. Two other people were present — we were about to make a whist four — and I was not best pleased that my private business should be known to them. However, Stoker is incurably ebullient and I comforted myself with the thought that men wouldn't gossip about my contract as women would.

'For four weeks twice nightly weekdays at £20 each week,' said Stoker triumphantly. 'Mind you, I visit these parts a lot; I know the men behind this Conquest Theatre venture. All very comfortable men: very prosperous Scarborough tradesmen.'

One of the other gentlemen, a Mr Dunning to whom I'd taken an immediate liking, said quietly: 'Count Dracula, would you like me to cast a professional eye over the Scarborough worthies' contract. I am a lawyer by profession.' He had a gentle voice with, I would judge, some kind of West Country accent.

'Dunning will charge you a fortune,' roared Stoker, but the other shook his head, smiling, and began to read with a practised eye.

The other man, named Harry Candler, asked sharply, 'These

comfortable men, do they Travel? Travel is my business.'

'Didn't know it was a business. Thought it was a pleasure. Always a pleasure when I travel to Paris: only know three Frog words but I always get what I want.' Stoker laughed immoderately as he spoke, and the thought crossed my mind that he was particularly enjoying his holiday because his wife — Florence, I think — had stayed behind in London.

'Travel's very much a business,' said Candler. 'Thomas Cook and his boy John Mason have made it a big one. And there's plenty of room for others like me: wouldn't take them on in Switzerland or Italy, nor in Egypt or the Holy Land, but the rest of Europe's an open oyster.'

I looked at him keenly and was about to pursue the conversation when Stoker resumed like a torrent. 'Oh, they're warm Scarborough men. There's Chopper the grocer and wine merchant, made a fortune selling half-casks of keeping butter and Dome Black Lead. There's Dowen, pretends he's a medical man; he's a sort of pharmaceutical chemist, sells gallons of Biggs' Sheep Dip and Cod Oil for harness, Professor Holloway's Pills, George's Pile and Gravel Pills, Bragg's Charcoal Biscuits, Hopp Bitters — "Remember Hopp Bitters is no vile drugged nostrum" — Thompson's Burdock Pills — "purify the foulest blood" — your blood need purifying, eh, Dracula?'

It is hard to take offence at Stoker, and anyway he was off again. 'And there's little Fraser: Hats and Gents Ready Mades Shop — "Tweed Caps from $3\frac{1}{2}$d, Tweed trousers from 1/6, Boys' Reefing Jackets with Velvet Collars from 6/6d." Then, next door he's got Millinery and Mantles for silly women, dolmans, mob caps, felt chip and straw bonnets, sealskins from 13/- a yard.' When Stoker had finished laughing uproariously Mr Dunning returned the contract to me — 'It looks quite in order' — and brought our attention back to the card table. Yet I was impressed by Stoker's writer's memory for small details, although as a whist player he is not of the standard of Mr Dunning and myself.

August 22nd

A fearful disaster on which I do not want to dwell. I simply got the most acute stage fright.

The theatre was very new and smart and smelled of paint and, increasingly of cigar smoke. The front rows and plush boxes were filled with ladies and gentlemen in the elaborate evening clothes to be found in big provincial towns. The pit, the back seats of the circle and the gallery were crammed full with the humbler orders.

My performance required no speech. The Master of Ceremonies brought people from the audience to examine my coffin from every angle – some banged it with great zeal – the 'Coffin from the Wreck' looked suitably macabre, Biro appeared most impressive (he had cleaned and pressed his brilliant Szekely livery and polished the buttons until they dazzled), and I strode on to the stage, bowed, and took up my appointed place in leisured and elegant style (it is rare for a Szekely to move clumsily).

Then, after the lid had closed and the applause died to an excited buzz of expectation, I lost my head. I cannot think why, for I am sure we Draculas are not a prey to claustrophobia.

My formulae for change have been crystal clear in my mind since Uncle Vlad first instructed me. Since then I have several times had to employ them quickly and under great pressure. But, somehow, this time I got them mixed up. When Biro opened the coffin again, with a tremendous flourish, instead of an empty void from which only a bat fluttered away, out stepped a huge wolf. As I suddenly realised what I had done, distress overwhelmed me, my eyes burned, my jaws opened, I groaned with dismay and stepped quickly forward holding out an apologetic paw.

The buzz and murmur fell to a dead and utter silence. But not for long. Those in the front seats rose in terror; men shouting, women screaming. Then they began to run, up the centre aisle, to the side exits, their panic almost instantly communicating itself throughout the entire theatre. The musicians in the orchestra pit, who only a few moments earlier had been giving the gentle background of airs from *The Sorcerer*, abandoned their instruments and disappeared in a series of noisy scuffles. I turned my head towards the Master of Ceremonies, hoping that he would exercise his mastery, only to see him vanish into the wings at breakneck speed, leaving only a make-up bow-tie behind him. At the back of the theatre people were fighting to get out, and there were sounds of collapsing seats and breaking doors and glass, mixed with the hubbub of terrified voices.

One voice I heard clearly, however. It said, 'I'll get a shot gun.' I immediately returned to the coffin, which Biro closed, and when I had resumed my normal appearance we both walked unnoticed through the deserted wings and left quietly by the stage door. As we returned pensively to the hotel it became obvious that fire brigade, ambulance and police were all hastening to the stricken theatre.

August 23rd

The Dailygraph has, of course, a long and rather hysterical story about last night's events. Although I rose late and remained in my room for a light breakfast, I determined to face the world just as usual. Biro valeted me with particular care and I descended to a small room which the hotel had put at my disposal to speak to the several people anxious to interview me (the hotel is being most helpful and the excellent woman at the reception desk told me that they were to vary their advertisements to 'Sir Henry Irving *and* Count Dracula have stayed here.'

An earnest reporter for *The Dailygraph* was the first person to come in. I was courteous but brief.

'Count Dracula, sir, yours must be one of the most

extraordinary and terrifying illusions in the history of the theatre.'

'I would hardly claim that.'

'£1,000 worth of damage, thirty people in hospital, including the Mayor, who is suffering from delusions — '

' — that is an occupational hazard —'

' — surely no illusionist has ever before created such panic? The Mayor, who was in the front row of the orchestra stalls, at present believes he is a sheep's entrails.'

I forbore to comment.

'The trombonist, who was even closer to you, has since bitten through the mouthpiece of his instrument, crying, "I've got the fangs! I've got the fangs!" '

I am not an aristocrat and a Balliol man for nothing. Smoothly I replied, 'You must remember that, however English my education and sympathies, I come from Central Europe, the heart and cockpit of our modern civilisation. These engaging and romantic mysteries and illusions are commonplace to us.'

'Who taught them to you?'

'My nanny,' I said firmly.

Mina came next, and her visit was brief and encouraging.

'Ooh, Dracula', she said, wide-eyed, 'there seems to be nothing you can't do. Aren't you the most marvellous man in the world? And can I come round and see you after dinner, usual arrangements?'

I answered affirmatively to both questions.

To my surprise, Mr Dunning the lawyer was next. He said: 'Outside, talking to that reporter, is Mr Dowen. He is the prosperous pharmacist whose signature is on your contract. I like you, Count Dracula: you're an excellent whist partner. Would you wish me to stay when he comes in? I think he will engage in some legal threats.'

Ah, I thought, yet another good Englishman. I gratefully accepted his offer and asked that Mr Dowen be shown in.

The pharmacist was obviously a vain man. He constantly combed back his dark and not very romantic — indeed rather dandruffy – locks, and his tone was hectoring rather than diplomatic.

'Now look here, Dracula,' he began.

'Pray, Mr Dowen, accord me my proper title, Count Dracula.'

'Well, Count Dracula, then. Let's not beat about the bush. Firstly, not one brass farthing of pay will you get from me and my fellow owners of the theatre. Secondly, we expect large compensation from you for the £2000 worth of damage and the sixty people in hospital as a result of your act.'

I was about to reply when Mr Dunning cleared his throat. 'Mr Dowen, I take it that you and your fellow tradespeople are insured in this matter?'

Combing back his forelock, he grudgingly admitted that this was so.

'Good. You certainly owe the Count a considerable debt of gratitude.'

Dowen made a sound of choked disagreement, and Mr Dunning continued severely, 'As a consequence of one illusion, however effective, in your theatre, there has been some injury and damage but happily no fatalities. Consider what a reality, the reality of a sudden fire, might have caused in a building so manifestly ill-equipped with exits. So check your exits, increase your emergency exits, be grateful that the Count has revealed this fearful weakness in your theatre which might cost you so many lives. It might,' he added, drily, 'even cost you a good deal of money.'

Dowen went pale, and Mr Dunning continued, 'Furthermore, the Count has fulfilled, and is willing to continue to fulfil, his side of your contract, a contract, which I have examined carefully. If it comes to the High Court – and, particularly, if it comes to the Court of Appeal – you wouldn't have a splint to stand on. You should therefore pay him the sum of £80 within the next twenty-eight days.'

'Doubtless to be used,' snarled Dowen, 'on buying tobacco and alcohol.'

'There are worse uses.' Mr Dunning turned to me: 'May we

now bid Mr Dowen good day?'

I agreed that we might and, after he had stamped out, Mr Dunning said shortly, 'He'll pay.'

'I would wish,' I said, 'when I receive the money, to pay it across to you, in gratitude for your kindness.'

'Thank you, no. But you may send ten guineas, no more, to a Central African mission which I shall name. I have been much concerned with Dr Livingstone, and am anxious to support missionary work in what was very much his area. And I look forward to the additional recompense of playing whist with you.'

August 28th

Attended what should have been a cheerful dinner party last night at the Westenras. Lucy looked decidedly better – 'I eat like a cormorant,' she declared, and she's certainly a somewhat greedy girl. Mina was absent, but that was because the Westenras think she has already returned to her husband, which she has not. Lucy's fiancé, the Hon. Arthur was present, and this at least ensured that several amusing people from good Yorkshire families, including Lord and Lady Cooper, made very agreeable conversations before dinner. The Hon. Arthur himself, always a dull dog, was even duller because of the news of the illness of his father, Lord Godalming. His brash friend, Quincey Morris, has an open manner and a veiled eye which appears to have made him deeply disliked in his native town of Dallas.

Van Helsing was accompanied by no less than three friends. The first, a very plump man who seemed to overflow his clothes, resembled one of those actors who play villainous Prussians in the melodramas at the Surrey or the Vic; his conversation was highly amusing, if in a rather sinister way. Ven Helsing addressed him as Georgie, and his jowled face seemed slightly familiar – then I recalled that he had been with Horrolds the day I dismissed him.

The second was English enough. He was introduced to me as

St George Fillerby, and yet I was instantly aware, from his darting and oddly lecherous eyes, that he was no more than one of Van Helsing's creatures. The third, Mrs Westenra told me in a happy flutter (for of course this was by far the grandest dinner party she had ever given) was Irma, Baroness Chnoupek. I know the *Almanach de Gotha* almost by heart (*Burke's Peerage and Baronetage*, too) and I was fairly sure that no such title existed and that the woman was an adventuress.

The episode at the Conquest Theatre was of course a leading subject for talk and comment. To my astonishment, and pleasure, my act seems to have produced much admiration. However, throughout the conversation I kept Van Helsing in the corner of my eye. He slipped into the dining room for a few moments and, after he had returned, I did the same. The quite elaborate setting of the table even included place cards, and I saw that I was between Georgie and Lady Grylle: the latter is an elderly lady but astonishingly well preserved and a thoroughly entertaining rattle. I could not immediately see that my enemy had set any trap for me but, as a precaution, I changed my chair with Georgie's.

This proved a wise step for when we went into dinner some minutes later and took our seats, Georgie immediately rose again with an agonised cry, then fell to the ground holding an ample buttock in a convulsive grasp. As Dr Seward hastened to his side in the commotion, my lightning glance noted a sharp projecting point in the seat of his chair: it was coated with a brown substance which I guessed to be curare.

Muttering, 'Where is my $C_2 HCL_3 OH_2O$?' Dr Seward quickly examined Georgie's skull and peered closely into his eyes. Lady Grylle said loudly, 'I think you are looking at the wrong end,' adding, more quietly, to me, 'That's the trouble with these head doctors, so limited.'

But even among all the confusion I kept watch on Van Helsing, fearing – rightly, it proved – his infinite resource. In an instant he was at my side, peering at Georgie and the Doctor, yet bringing something from his full pocket which – I noticed that his left hand was now heavily gauntleted – he transferred to mine. Then I felt something, some living creature, stir where the pocket pressed my side.

I did not plunge my hand in to ascertain what it was, but instantly seized a table napkin and dropped to my knees beside Dr Seward.

'Quick, quick,' I cried, 'I saw this once before in Wallachia: I may be able to save him. The napkin will keep his jaws and teeth apart as with epileptics – ' I suited action to my words with both hands, receiving a nasty nip from Georgie in the process – 'and we need a tourniquet. Fillerby, Fillerby, this instant please, there's a silk handkerchief in my right-hand pocket which will perfectly serve.'

What Fillerby brought out proved to be a small, cross krait. After biting him twice the snake wriggled away; its venom expended, it was shortly afterwards killed by the Westenras' tabby.

George and Fillerby now lay side by side and after a few moments Dr Seward was able, quite authoritatively, to pronounce them both dead.

The dinner party was now in some disarray. Although the country folk, familiar of course with a variety of dead animals slaughtered in sport, were comparatively unconcerned (I saw Lady Cooper making notes of the events), Lucy was having the vapours and Mrs Westenra was crying helplessly, 'Whatever shall we do now? Whatever shall we do?'

The admirable Lady Grylle took charge. 'First, make certain that the soup is still hot: I detest tepid soup. Then put the bodies in the drawing room for the time being. There is no blood, so the carpet will not be harmed. Remove two chairs and settings–it will make comfortably more room for us all – and let us commence dinner. I, for one, am in great need of my dinner.'

The enforced rearrangement meant that the admirable Lady Grylle was to my left, my enemy at my right hand. Lady Grylle turned from soup to oysters. 'Terribly expensive they're becoming. 8d a dozen and I do *so* enjoy them.'

I congratulated her on her coolness and self-possession at our decimated dinner party.

'It quite takes me back,' she said cheerfully, peppering her oysters with enthusiasm, 'to my days in India. I was in Lucknow, you know, during the siege. Before General Havelock relieved us — such a dreary man he was, dear Sir James Outram was much more clubbable — before the first Relief we'd sometimes sit down to a meal and between soup and sweet, if the mutineers were keeping up a hot fire, we might lose nearly half our number.'

She polished off the oysters and moved on to the entrée. 'Ah, yes,' she said reflectively, 'happy days, happy days.'

They were hardly my idea of happiness, but I did not reply as I was again watching Van Helsing's left hand intently. And, sure enough, as the claret was poured, impenetrably dark red in the thick cut-crystal glass, his hand moved through the air and the surface of the wine in my glass trembled: a small capsule or pellet had been adroitly added.

Now I had time for reflection. I toyed with my glass; several times I raised it to my lips, only to lower it to resume conversation with Lady Grylle. I could sense my enemy's excitement surging and falling away in frustration.

Then I rose, walked round the table and knelt, with a gallant air, beside his confederate, Irma. I was conscious that eyes were on me, Van Helsing's questioning, Lady Grylle's disapproving.

'Countess,' I said, 'Countess Irma, I am convinced that, through our mutual cousinage with the Bohemian Chnoupeks, we are related. We should drink a toast to each other as cousins meeting for the first, but certainly not the last time.'

With that I intertwined my arm with hers as I had seen courting peasant boys and girls do in taverns in Bistritz, so that each, affectionately, drank from the other's glass. We drank.

This time Lady Grylle took entire control. From her Indian Mutiny experience she declared Irma to be dead and then said, briskly, '*Three* bodies in the drawing room is really too much. Someone might trip and sprain an ankle. I think they should be removed below stairs: the men in the kitchen, Irma in the scullery. Yes, Irma quite definitely in the scullery.'

I made to help the other men in this task, but Lady Grylle held my sleeve. Led by Quincey Morris, who was handicapped by large Texan feet and a large intake of wine, they sounded to be making heavy weather of it.

'Such a flawless natural complexion. Its upkeep requires a great deal of effort and *maquillage*. She wasn't really your cousin, was she?'

I fell into a fit of non-committal coughing.

'Exactly,' said Lady Grylle. 'Didn't think she was for a moment. You're an excellent young man, Count Dracula. Would you be so very kind as to carve some meat for me? I'm especially partial to crackling.'

When I came back she said, 'Thank you. And in return let me give you this. I saw it bulging in the pocket of that dull Dutchman. He was in quite a state over the demise of your improbable cousin, and I thought he'd be better without it. No, I didn't tell him.' I found I was holding a revolver, and hastily put it where the krait had been.

Later, with some rather difficult adieux made, I began to stroll back to my hotel, which was but a short distance away, reflecting among things that if the Westenras really were to move upwards in the social world they would need to stop placing saucers of milk by the front door. The night was soft, the moon high and strong; suddenly in the drive before me stood Van Helsing, his expression well-nigh demented with rage.

'Three — three of my best people,' he hissed. 'But they shall be avenged, and *now*.'

He plunged his hand into his pocket, searching wildly and in vain, and glared at me yet more savagely. I wished that I had the faintest idea how his revolver, now bulging in my pocket, actually worked. Neither Dr Jowett nor K had ever explained this to me.

'Nor shall you escape again,' he snarled. In his hand was his evening cane, and as he tugged at it the moonlight's glint revealed it as a swordstick. Although he was having some difficulty in its unsheathing I realised that within a second or two I might be run through the heart. He dropped to one knee to pull it clean and then – and how I blessed the English with their saucers of milk and love of hedgehogs – gave a scream of pain and clutched his punctured leg. As he rose I sprang forward: two blows, of which my mentor Henry Brute could only have been proud, and he lay unconscious. But as I considered whether I should find out how his revolver worked and kill him with that, or whether I should spit him with his own swordstick, Dr Seward and Quincey Morris came down the drive together: the latter, inappropriately for a Southerner I thought, singing 'John Brown's Body' at the top of his voice.

The opportunity was gone, and I left my enemy cradled in the hydrangeas and walked gently home.

August 30th

I had arranged to have a talk before returning to London with Mr Candler, whose business is travel. I took Biro with me.

'Would you,' I said directly, 'think of taking Candler's Tours into the very heart of Europe? For example, to my own incomparable beautiful and romantic Transylvania?'

He looked doubtful. 'I'd think about it. Our English ladies of today are very adventurous, more so than our menfolk, I believe. D'you know, Count – ' Candler was warming to his theme – 'you'll find English ladies, in the heaviest clothing under the hottest suns, walking, riding horses, mules, donkeys, jennets. They're afraid of nobody: they'll stand up to hoteliers, brigands, even dragomen. They want to go to strange new places – and tell their neighbours about it afterwards. With sketches.'

'Keeping ahead of the Joneses,' I said (the English have some odd idioms).

'And of the Higginbottoms, too. There's a lot of money, new brass, in Lancashire and Yorkshire nowadays. And they don't mind spending it.'

'So Transylvania wouldn't frighten them?'

'No. But the accommodation would. They can bear discomfort but not dirt, and the inns and post houses of that region are plain, simple — and very dirty. If I persuaded English travellers to go I should afterwards get endless complaints and demands for refunds, supported by certificates from their family physicians, saying that they had been bitten by fleas, attacked by ticks, penetrated by lice. That their valises had been devoured by huge mice and bold rats. That's the stumbling block.'

'And if they could stay in a great castle? Say in Castle Dracula, near Bistritz?'

It is always interesting to watch the reaction of an English businessman to an idea that might bring in money.

'Go on, please,' said Mr Candler, taking out a large notebook.

'My Castle is huge and romantic. A hundred people can sleep there; two hundred eat in the great Banqueting Hall. Our kitchens are vast. And now, as Biro has reminded me, it stands sad and empty.'

'And, forgive me, dirty?'

'And rather dirty. But that can quickly be changed. Labour, like life, is cheap in Transylvania, and our peasants are numerous and loyal. If there was to be some profit for them, every room would be scrubbed and garnished, tonnes of Keatings put to work, the silver and the chandeliers brought to brilliance. The cockroaches could be banished from the kitchens and sculleries and butteries. They could be filled with the smells of delicious and unusual foods — foods that the Joneses and Higginbottoms have never tasted before.'

Mr Candler's pencil squeaked. 'And how might the tourists pass their days?'

'Visit the wonderful countryside and the mountains. There are horses and mules to ride, carriages and calèches to hire for a song. The summers are long and hot; there could be bathing in the Great Black Lake behind the stables.'

'Bathing. *Mixed* bathing?' Candler sounded doubtful.

'There are craftsmen among our peasants. Carpenters can

107

quickly contrive separate bathing huts. Then there are gypsy bands, gypsy violinists with their wild melodies. And country fairs and spectacles.'

'There might be a really good impal — ' Biro stopped as I kicked him swiftly beneath the table.

'It's worth thinking about,' said Mr Candler.

Biro looked up, rubbing his knee joint. 'And they could go to the wolf pens.'

'The what?'

'Wolf pens. We have packs of the finest and fiercest wolves in Europe. Or even in Russia.' Biro was warming to his theme. 'Great, savage, glowering, slavering, grey brutes, they are — '

'That's enough,' said Candler, 'I'm off.'

'Where to?'

'To Bistritz. You'd better give me a letter. Be in touch with you directly I return.'

He rose and shook hands: as he reached the door he checked and said, a little wistfully, 'Pity. I suppose they don't have any good impalings any more?'

September 1st

It is very agreeable to be back in London, although of course the season has not begun and anyone who is anybody is out of town. Invitations were awaiting me in Half Moon Street to go to Cotterell Castle, Stansgate Towers and other rich homes, but it was especially pleasant to relax with dear Mr Drummond and Stock, and to tell them of my latest bout with Van Helsing.

I had never seen Mr Drummond so pleased and excited: he actually bit through the stem of his meerschaum as I unfolded my tale. 'Gad, Dracula, you've done England much service in ridding us of those three scoundrels.'

'Remember,' said Stock, 'what the infamous Georgie did to poor Basil and poor Reuben?'

They were silent for a moment; then Mr Drummond added,

'And what Irma did to you.'

While Stock blushed, he continued: 'K will be very pleased with you. You may expect commendation from the very highest quarters. And I'm sure his confidence in you is now such that you'll be asked to take part in another, and highly confidential, matter.'

'Pray tell me about it.'

'My lips are sealed. And, by the way, the current codeword is Trotsch.'

September 10th

There is good news from my Uncle Vlad who, with wise severity, is quickly restoring the fortunes of my great estate. His letter tells me how diligently the peasants are working – 'you would almost think they were afraid of me' – and it encloses a draft for a substantial sum. A grudging note has come from Dowen, the Scarborough pharmacist, enclosing the sum of £80 (I'm convinced that Mr Dunning will reach the top of his profession), and Mina arrived this morning with an envelope from her husband Harker.

'He has no idea that we have done more than pass a few words together,' she said; adding with a real and mounting indignation, 'But do you know, Dracula darling, that the wretch has clearly been unfaithful to me while I was away. There are evidences of Another Woman in the bedroom. How wicked, cruel and wanton men are. What evening can we meet again?'

Harker's note contained a cheque for 120 guineas, the first quarter's rent in advance for my great Piccadilly house. I reviewed my reviving financial situation and wrote a note to Mr Dunning, asking if he would find and rent two small, adjacent apartments in the centre of town, one for my use, the other for Mrs Merry and her daughter. This I entrusted to Biro: as I explained its contents his face lit up with pleasure. The thought occurred to me that if Erika and Mina should arrive simultaneously at the apartment for my use, he would have to exercise all his ingenuity; but I thought it wiser not to mention this until later.

And I have decided to pay a visit to my prompt-paying Piccadilly tenants tomorrow.

September 17th

Today I strolled round the corner of Half Moon Street and down Piccadilly to make myself known to my tenants. I felt this necessary since Jonathan Harker's envelope had also contained a covering letter strongly urging me *not* to visit them.

It appeared that my tenants were an affectionate family, for as I went up the familiar steps a silver-haired man of distinguished appearance, evidently the *pater familias*, was saying good bye to a young and pretty girl with an exceedingly warm kiss. It seemed also to be a large family especially blessed on the distaff side, for when I entered the hall I glimpsed several other young ladies. It was chilly this morning and the thought struck me that none of them was as warmly clad as prudence would have suggested.

A maid approached: she had a decidedly perter manner than I would have wished. However, she quickly ushered me in to her mistress, who proved to be indeed the ample and richly coloured lady whom I'd earlier glimpsed.

'Delighted to welcome you here,' she said effusively. 'Is there any one of my dear girls you would prefer to see?'

Responding to my bewildered look, she continued, 'You're new, aren't you. Many of our new gentlemen come on a personal recommendation.'

I laid my card on her table. 'Hardly new. I own this property, and you're my tenant.'

She looked startled. 'Oh, Count Dracula. Mr Harker said you wouldn't ever ... anyway, where are my manners. Pray be seated. Perhaps a glass of Madeira?'

I accepted and, although it was Bual rather than Sercial, it proved perfectly palatable. She drank two glasses one after the other, poured a third, and said more confidently, 'I'm Mrs Roza. My husband was a Maltese gentleman. He was on the shipping side.'

'Was? Then that gentleman I passed on the steps is not your husband?'

'You mean Lord ... well, his name is of no consequence. Certainly he isn't my husband.' She laughed inordinately, and the phrase 'shaking with laughter' took on a new significance.. When her rippling mirth had subsided, Mrs Roza said, 'Well, I certainly didn't expect to see you here, Count Dracula. But of course you're a most welcome surprise. Now, would you like to inspect our business? It is, of course, of the highest class.'

I was more bewildered than ever. 'Business, what business?'

'Well,' she beamed at me, 'I always call it a House of Joy. I think that's a lovely description: so true, really.'

My silence was so extended that she enquired anxiously, 'Are you all right, Count Dracula? Is there anything you'd like?'

'Another glass of Madeira,' I said faintly.

After we'd both had another glass, I said, 'So this is a brothel.'

'Oh, no, no. Mr Harker and I agreed that we'd never use a common word like that. No, a House of Joy. A House of Pleasure.'

'But not in my house. Absolutely *not*,' I said with increasing firmness, 'in my house. You'll have to go.'

Mrs Roza pleaded and cajoled and wept. She brought out another bottle of Madeira, but I remained courteously adamant.

'I'm sorry, madam. You may remain here until the end of the quarter. If you have difficulty in finding alternative accommodation, you may stay here a further month. But after that you must go.'

'Oh dear,' she cried, 'we'll never find such good accommodation. This is the perfect site. I always used to say to Mr Horrolds this would be the perfect site, and it is. The business is increasing by leaps and bounds, jumping ahead.'

'I hope you will have similar prosperity elsewhere.'

'It wouldn't be the money?' she demanded. 'I'll pay more money, much more. Forgive me asking, Count, but how much money are you getting from that Mr Harker?'

'120 guineas a quarter.'

'That's just half what I'm paying him. We had a little, well, arrangement. I promised I'd never tell you, but then he said I'd never see you anyway, and I'm a bit tiddly, and that Harker's made such a mess of it all – ' She wept noisily, and then tried again. 'And if you wanted to be a client it would be absolutely free. On the house. Our best girls – please see our best girls.'

She rang the bell imperiously, and ordered the maid: 'Bring in Janine and Helene.'

Janine and Helene proved to be young and excessively pretty. Instructed by Madame Roza to tell me about their business they did so in a flow of artless prattle which was decidedly entertaining. But I noticed that their chatter never included names.

'Now, Tuesdays, sir,' said Janine, 'nothing at all happens to us, nothing at all, really.'

'How do you mean?'

'Well, in the morning it's all the whips and canes, you see, and in the afternoon they come with photographic equipment.'

'We get quite a lot of reverend gentlemen, you know clergymen and priests and that,' said Helene.

'They often like us to pose as faeries.'

'Naked faeries,' said Janine, firmly.

'And then we're off Thursdays. That's Men Only.'

I was about to ask for an explanation of Men Only when there were sounds of fearful altercation outside. Then the door was kicked open and a middle-aged man, very well dressed and very drunk, stumbled in. 'Look here, Roza,' he shouted, 'you know me. I've been coming to you for long enough. With my friend Algernon. Every Thursday I come, every damned Thursday. And there's Larry and Harry waiting for me, Lord Arthur Somerset. And here I am, and here they aren't. Just these horrid, horrid girls.'

112

He looked balefully at Janine and Helene, who looked back at him without enthusiasm. I wondered whether to knock him down or no.

'So where this Thursday are Larry and Harry, Harry and Larry, eh?'

'They're here every Thursday. Today's Wednesday,' said Madame Roza.

'Wednesday is it? Today's Wednesday. Right, I'll be back the day after tomorrow.'

He departed unsteadily, and subsequent noises suggested that he had fallen down the steps as he left. I thought it time to leave myself. 'You may stay here another four months. My solicitor, Mr Dunning, will call to obtain from you an affidavit about Harker's behaviour. Madame Roza, mesdemoiselles, it has been a pleasure to meet you.'

October 3rd

John Seward had invited a small party of people he had met at Whitby to look over his lunatic asylum near Purfleet – Arthur Holmwood, Mr Dunning and myself. Seward showed us round, helped by a medical friend of his, a Patrick Hennessey, who was very jolly and slightly drunk: Holmwood and Seward, who were both extremely glum, looked daggers at him. I do not like Holmwood (who has just succeeded to the title of Lord Godalming), still less do I like his friends, but I could not but feel sorry for the poor fellow. For his affianced, the consumptive Lucy Westenra, died just a fortnight ago, and I gather there were distressing scenes at the funeral and afterwards. I thought Lucy a tiresome girl, but there is no doubt that Arthur was much in love with her.

Mr Dunning took the keenest and most careful interest, but I find the spectacle of ranting lunatics, as of democratic politicians, sad and distasteful. I found exception in a man called Ronald Renfield. He must be about sixty, but very strong and savage

113

looking. I gather that he insists on eating insects, dead or alive, and made a note to send him a few boxes of crystallised locusts. This evidently was the patient in whom, according to Mina, our host Seward is almost obsessively interested.

I don't think Seward is very intelligent, but he seems to work hard and correspond widely; he even knows an old friend of my dear, late Father's, Dr Arminius of Buda-Pesth. Renfield evidently fascinates him; indeed we were all astonished when the poor creature turned to Arthur and said in a very quiet and dignified way: 'I know you. You're Godalming's boy, ain't you? I remember your uncle well, seconded him when he was put up for some Club, the Windham or the Diogenes, I think.'

'I can't remember. Was he − was he not blackballed?' Holmwood was obviously taken aback.

'Blackballed!' cried Renfield. 'Blackballed! Have you never seen a pile of caviare?'

Then an even stranger thing occurred. Renfield looked fully at me and shouted violently 'Lord, Lord. Master, Master.'

I found this not unpleasing, but he went on shouting, 'You must be a Dracula, a Dracula. And if you are here, She, She, must be near!'

'Who do you mean?' I asked sharply. A sudden disagreeable thought struck me. 'You don't by any chance mean Shirley Dracula?'

I was thoroughly put out. We are a close family and blood is thicker than water, but Shirley has a distressing way of implying that she is a sort of family chieftain. Roy finds this decidedly trying, and if Uncle Vlad should ever learn of it, his wrath would be terrible. Hers was very much a cadet branch.

Renfield made no direct answer but fell to his knees before me crying, 'She is coming, She is near, oh, where is She?'

He was still shouting away to this effect when the attendants, with considerable difficulty, removed him. The whole business was most unfortunate and left me greatly miffed. Affairs are perfectly in order provided they are discreet and don't give rise

114

to distress and unseemly noise: the affairs of the Un-Dead – for I can only assume that Shirley and Renfield have earlier enjoyed some intimate relationship – should be conducted with a special discretion. Otherwise, however unimaginable it may seem, the Dracula family might come to have a bad name.

The whole thing was made odder when I returned to our overnight hotel and found a message awaiting me: it had come by means of telegraph, and was from Shirley. Apparently she was in the neighbourhood for a conference, had intended joining me at the asylum (quite unasked) when it was over; but would not now do so since her discussions – on Preventing the Spread of Education – had gone on longer than expected.

So Renfield was right. Some aspect of their affair must have bitten very deeply into his heart and mind.

October 7th

Among the several letters awaiting me in Half Moon Street this morning was one from Bell-Mountain, reproaching me for not visiting Cotterell Castle and the rural delights of Chipping Stoat. This is very difficult to answer for I cannot of course tell the dear fellow anything of the secret work in which I am engaged, and he evidently feels hurt. His family has indeed extended me much hospitality, both at the Castle and at their Belgrave Square house which they open up rather infrequently.

It was there however that I met Mr Gladstone. He and the Earl, as I recollect, had little in common, for while WEG wanted to save all fallen women, the Earl appeared only to want the best ones saved for him. And of course I met HRH the Prince of Wales there, a very lively man if somewhat foreign-sounding – and a splendid whist player.

Another letter was a grateful note from Mrs Merry:

'The flowers are all open and the sky is blue
Me and my little Pam heap blessings all on you.'

I showed this to Biro, who commented:

'My dear Pam, Master, Count, I feel
Isn't so little but rather is bountiful.'

I think Biro is a much better artist than poet, but that there may be the basis for a successful poem there: perhaps I should mention it to Alfred Austin.

There was an invitation from Roy Dracula to dine at the Marlborough Club. I have accepted this with alacrity since my evenings with him, which I always enjoy, have been fewer of late. He is spending a good deal of time in Scotland nowadays: presumably for reasons of profit since his comment to me about the Scotch, particularly the Glaswegians, was, 'They remind me of those dreadful serfs on the Wallachian estates in the 1760s.'

And there was a summons to Goodwin's Court, which I am answering this very evening. I shall wait until tomorrow to write about it.

October 8th

K congratulated me very warmly on my actions in Beograd and Whitby, and then turned to our new business. He was drinking port but not sucking lozenges, and spoke quietly. 'Deuced odd one, this. Down in Spitalfields – Dorset Road, Hanbury Street, round there – several whores been killed.'

It was difficult to feel any surprise at this.

'Four of 'em killed within a few days. Throats cut from left to right. They're worried down in Whitechapel; Scotland Yard, too. Helpful feller there called Inspector Abberline.'

K paused, scribbled a note and shouted for his secretary. 'Miss

Buckle. Take that round well before 3.30. To my usual bookmaker.'

Turning to me again, he continued: 'Now, the trouble is that young Prince Eddy has been going to those parts. D'you know him?'

'I've met the Duke of Clarence at a levee. Also his younger brother, the Duke of York.'

'Did you like him?'

'I'm afraid not. The younger brother George seems much more agreeable.'

'Don't think anyone likes Eddy. Except his mother, Princess Alix. And it's not only his awful little moustache,' K said gloomily. 'Anyway, he's been goin' down there. You can guess why. And we think someone is killing the trulls he's been involved with to get a real Royal scandal going.'

'Why?'

'Get the gutter press on about it. Home and abroad. Rock the Royal Family; upset the establishment; do real damage to the national reputation. Just what our enemies want. That's what Salisbury thinks. More important,' added K, 'that's what I think.'

'Do you, then, want me to watch the Prince's interests?'

'No, no. The Prince of Wales has already arranged for that. Man called Holmes.'

'I know him slightly: he has a most able and intelligent friend, with excellent medical experience in Afghanistan, a Dr Watson.'

'Tiresome chap, Holmes. Drugs, I think. Glad you know him. Easier to work together.'

'And what is my work?'

'Perhaps you can guess. Who hates this country? Who has unlimited Russian money to hire agents to work against this country? Who but Van Helsing?'

'Ah.'

'He's finding the tarts that Eddy's had; having them killed; putting it about that Eddy killed 'em. Of course, he couldn't kill anything save a conversation. But it's a clever trick. Mind you,' K went on, 'if we stop it this time they'll try the same thing in a

117

year or two, mark my words.'

'So my instructions are – ?'

'Off to Whitechapel tomorrow morning. You've bested Van Helsing twice: beat him again. The current codeword is Gunge.'

October 9th

Events have moved rapidly.

It was barely dawn when a ferocious knocking sounded at our front door. Mr Drummond, with his years of training, answered it immediately and brought in a panting policeman. 'Can you come immediately, Count Dracula? There's been another Whitechapel murder, and I've a hansom waiting outside to take you there urgent.'

The cabbie at first seemed anxious to drive very slowly eastwards, shouting a series of general knowledge questions at us and providing the answers before there was a chance to reply. However, P.C. Mizen, in terms which reminded me strongly of my good 'Enery, persuaded him to shut up and drive fast, and in no time at all we joined a sombre group in a roped-off section off Millers Court. After a while I learned – mostly from the shouts of assembled journalists kept outside the ropes – that those present included the Assistant Commissioner at Scotland Yard, James Monro, and with him Inspector Abberline, Inspector McWilliam of the City of London Detective Department, Detective Sergeant Thick and P.C. Neil: they were clustered around the body of some poor trull whose throat had been savagely cut. I must confess to a moment of faintness at the unbridled profusion of so much blood.

Dr Watson and Mr Holmes, evidently arrived from Baker Street a few seconds earlier, were approaching the grisly remains together: Dr Watson dropped to one knee saying, 'You know my methods, Holmes,' while his companion carefully surveyed the scene, first with the naked eye and then with a huge magnifying glass. He was wearing an extraordinary tweed fore-

118

and-aft hat with earpieces – the kind of hat sometimes sported by English gentlemen when stalking deer in Scotland.

After some moments, Sherlock Holmes said, 'You will observe that the throat was cut *clockwise.*'

'Surely that would depend,' I ventured in the ensuing silence, 'on whether it was cut from the front or from behind?'

He glowered at me, withdrew to his hansom cab and opened a large, black, oddly shaped box which I assumed to contain the essentials of a master detective's trade. In fact it held a violin. This he took from the case and, removing his pipe and his cap, began to play selections from Gilbert and Sullivan.

The English are indeed a wonderfully kind and generous people, for I soon noticed, before my attention was sharply diverted, that even in this squalid and decaying quarter of the great City, people were dropping small coins into his upturned hat.

But what diverted my attention was the sound of a voice, a voice now as familiar as it was evil; Van Helsing's voice.

He had not seen me, but was talking animatedly to two men pressed against the roped barrier.

'My name,' he said to them, 'is George Hutchinson. The police won't listen; they don't want to listen. But you two gentlemen of the press will want to listen, and to write what I have to say. Because I saw the murderer plain as he left the body. *And I know who he is.*'

The two journalists were galvanised: 'For God's sake tell us,' they cried as one.

'Who are you, what are your papers and will you pay?'

Both declared that they would pay improbably large sums, and Van Helsing dropped his voice. But I was close behind him now. 'I must warn you that what I saw was adverse to the Monarchy. Would that deter you?'

The first journalist stiffened. 'I am the famous freelance, Paul Trott. I hate the monarchy much more than Labouchère. Anything you tell me against them, I'll get printed. I was in these parts, with Louis Diemschutz of the Socialist Club in Berners

Street, to talk of this very thing.'

'Can't be quite so sure,' said the second man. 'I'm Harry Dale. I'm an investigative journalist, a very famous investigative journalist, and I couldn't print anything until it was absolutely confirmed.'

'I absolutely confirm,' said Van Helsing, 'that I saw the murderer and that it was unmistakably the Queen's grandson, Prince Eddy. He wreaks his wicked way with these unfortunates and then rips them to death.'

'That's enough confirmation for me,' cried Harry. 'The three of us must go to The Britannia pub, away from this gang: knock them up, get drinks, get all this down in detail — '

At this moment, Van Helsing saw and instantly recognised me. Shouting hoarsely, he pointed directly: four burly men elbowed through the ruck and made towards me. I turned towards my police allies — but they had gone: the body and the distinguished detectives had moved on, I could no longer hear Holmes playing nor see the comforting figure of Dr Watson. I took to my heels with my enemies in hot pursuit.

I moved fast yet I hope gracefully down the mean streets. But my flight was desperate; my allies gone, Van Helsing and his four ruffians pounding behind me. There was not enough time for transformation to a bat, and a grey wolf in Commercial Street seemed inappropriate.

Rounding a corner, momentarily out of my pursuers' view, I saw an open door and above it the sign 'Chinese Dentist.' Slamming and bolting the door, I bounded up the stairs into a waiting room. There was, however, no waiting: a young man in a white smock, so starched and ironed that it later abraded my sensitive skin, instantly took my arm, hastened me through to his dental chair, and in a moment had me both seated and strapped down. He left me for a moment and, straining my ears, I heard him talking into a kind of speaking tube: 'My sister, come up quickly from the laundry. A patient is here. In the chair.' He returned: I struggled unavailingly, able to say very little as he had wedged my mouth with what appeared to be a small ball-peine hammer.

'What do you think is wrong with you?'

'Nothing.'

'Ah, that's what they always say. Now let me have a good look.'

He did so, aided by his sister, a very pretty girl in a dazzling white smock who stood behind him striking lucifers to shed light on his search: her hand was a little tremulous and I could hear and smell one of my whiskers singeing.

'Well,' he said in a disappointed voice, 'you seem to have perfect teeth. Very good condition and absolutely normal.'

I thought they could tell him differently in Harley Street but was unable to say so. I was wondering, too, if Van Helsing had really lost my trail.

'Tell you what I'll do. I'll scale your teeth, they could do with that. Tartaric acid, you know.'

I nodded assent, managing to articulate, 'Quick.'

'Certainly, that will be 2/6d.'

I nodded again.

'In advance.'

As his sister removed 3/- from my pocket and carefully returned 6d change, he asked my birth date.

When I told him he opened a vast broom cupboard in the corner of the surgery. Pasted to the inside of the opened door were curious charts with triangles and circles: more encouragingly there was a small array of dental certificates.

'I can't treat you very well,' he said, setting to work painfully but not lethally, 'since you are a wood snake of the hours of the monkey and I an earth pig of the hours of the tiger, so that we are incompatible.'

'Uck,' I said.

'Now had it been my sister — sorry about the blood, I'd just swallow it if I were you — you would have been a compatible patient. She is a metal rat of the hours of the dragon.'

At last he was finished, and I stood at the top of the stairs shaking hands with his sister, since this appeared to be the custom of the practice. Suddenly a powerful kick shattered the small bolt of the outer door, and Van Helsing's remorseless tones reached us with fearful clarity. 'Right. Two of you at this end, the others at the far end of the street. He's in one of these houses, and I shall flush him out. When he breaks cover he's to be killed. You understand.'

An alarming number of voices agreed that they did.

There was time for a transformation, but the Chinese girl reacted quicker than me to the situation: in a moment, without her brother even seeing, I was standing in the big broom cupboard. Close to, it appeared that the certificates were all for ballroom dancing.

I applied my eye to a knot hole. Van Helsing appeared cautiously in the doorway, great bushed eyebrows over the cruel questing eyes. To my huge relief the dentist seized his arm in a professional grasp and before the Dutchman could protest had him seated – and strapped – in the chair.

The protests, when they came, were of a dreadful vehemence. The dentist was unmoved. 'Now, sir,' he said, 'Don't spoil it now. You've plucked up the courage to come – very brave of you – now let's go through with it.'

He inserted the ball-peine hammer; Van Helsing's teeth seemed almost to strike sparks from the metal as he strained and gnashed in vain. 'My word, but there *is* a lot needs doing. I'm afraid it may hurt a good deal, but you'll be ever so grateful to me in a week's time when you're over the worst. Well, perhaps in a month's time.'

The girl opened the cupboard door and signalled that we should go.

'I always like payment in advance. And I'm afraid it'll have to be £1; there's really so much to be done. I expect you keep your money in your right pocket?'

He plunged his hand in, and brought out a small curved dagger and an ugly-looking revolver, which he placed carefully in the enamel spitting bowl. 'Here we are. Your wallet's in the left pocket. Just the pound, and then we can get down to work.'

I stepped across the room and gathered the revolver which I thrust into my cape pocket. I nodded to the dentist, who seemed only mildly surprised at my reappearance. Knowing that (save for the caking blood at the top of the gums) my teeth had never been whiter, I bowed to Van Helsing and gave him a courtly smile.

He seemed almost to burst. His face and neck suffused to a dark mottled red, yet with a yellowish tinge, much like an unripe loganberry. He struggled maniacally, but the dentist had obviously anticipated desperate and terrified patients and the straps held. The hammer in his mouth interfered with my understanding of what he was saying; as his sister and I slipped into the waiting room I heard the dentist's soothing tones: 'Now then, let's start on the easy ones first. I've got my small pliers ...'

As she closed the door I said quickly, 'But surely I'm still trapped? There's no back door or window.'

'No – ' she was very tranquil – 'we go down the shute to the laundry. Then through the laundry basement to the basement of Chi Minh, the Hygienic Pastrycook. I fear his shop is very filthy, but it has a back door to a different street. My brother will keep the gentleman for quite a time: I think you will soon be safely home.'

'Your name, pray?'

'Nancy Lee Gan.'

'Miss Lee Gan,' I said, as we approached Chi Minh's odorous backdoor, 'time presses now, but later I shall express my gratitude more fully. I cannot expect that ever again will my life be saved by a lady so charming and graceful.'

October 14th

K sent for me again today.

Biro is so clever at his drawing. I had described one of Van Helsing's roughs, whom I had seen closely, and after a short while and some correction he produced a remarkable likeness, which I gave to Mr Drummond for onward transmission.

Now K said; 'Well done again. Police picked up that feller, and his known associate. From your chap's drawing, as well as a description from Dr Watson.'

'I thought he and Holmes had gone?'

'Not really. Holmes had gone off, that's what. Talking to his brother Mycroft the other day – having a glass in his Pall Mall lodging, actually – and he's worried about Sherlock.'

'In what way?'

'Well, I thought he was on cocoa. But no, Mycroft says it's cocaine. Racketty, y'know. Good thing he's got John Watson to keep him on the rails.'

Both Mr Drummond and I expressed our respect for Dr Watson's abilities.

'Now, Dracula, d'ye know just what happened to Van Helsing? Out of action for quite a while, I hear. Seems he's lost all his teeth. How does a feller lose all his teeth, eh?'

I told them, and it seemed to give much pleasure. Mr Drummond said: 'That was your third round with him. The next meeting may prove the final count.' He flushed and added, 'Sorry, Dracula.'

K said, 'You deserve some furlough. I've paid a draft to your bank. Go and enjoy yourself.'

'How about the Whitechapel business: do you want me for that any more?'

'Stopped for a while. Stopped 'em stone dead. We're pleased. Van Helsing toothless, two of the actual murderers arrested; make a great song and dance of charging them. The suspicion's off poor Prince Eddy. Don't say they won't try the same trick again in a year or two, though. No doubt there'll be more sensational Whitechapel murders. So — ' K looked sharply at me — 'any idea where you want to take your holiday?'

October 15th

Yesterday I couldn't tell K where I would go. Today I know; a letter from Transylvania from the travel man Mr Candler has determined it for me.

'My dear Count,' he wrote, 'is there any chance of your visiting Castle Dracula shortly? I will be here for another three weeks. I think you'll be pleased and surprised at how much has been done. Our first visitors have already come and gone, and I am confident of profit and success for us both. I have had the privilege of meeting your Uncle, the Prince Vlad, who has proved infinitely kind and helpful. But I would like you to see for yourself some of our achievements and our problems.'

I spent a farewell evening with Mr Drummond and James Stock. The latter, deeply tanned, was just returned from some mission in the Caribbean. 'Did you ever learn,' he asked me, 'what happened to your disastrous bailiffs, Tomas and Niklaus?'

'No word of them has reached my Uncle or me.'

'Then I wonder if it could be the same. Little island of St Toucan, near Haiti, was there for a few hours on my last mission. Used to be a prosperous little spot; employed two strange bounders from somewhere like Hungary as economic advisers; whole little place promptly goes bust.'

'It sounds to be the same. I wonder where they'll turn up next.'

Mrs Merry, all agog that, with my recovering fortunes we will soon be returning to the Piccadilly house, was solicitous about my journey —

'If east you go from climate western
Pray, master, always keep your silken vest on.'

125

I made my extremely separate farewells to Erika and Mina, and also to Nancy Lee Gan. Biro brought her to Half Moon Street in a cab, and I was able to express my gratitude for her courage and resource with the gift of a fine jade bracelet. We talked easily and at length and indeed seem highly compatible. We bade each other *au revoir* in the properest manner; and yet I strongly sense that she shares some of the tastes and inclinations of Miss Walton and Mrs Harker.

October 20th

Our railway journey completed, and settled with a hamper in the calèche for the drive to the Castle, Biro said abruptly, as if fearing my refusal, 'I would like to marry Pam when we all return to the great Piccadilly house.'

After I had, gladly, given my consent, he went on rather nervously, 'And, Master, what about you? Will you marry?'

This was hardly a servant's business, but the concern on his honest face was so obvious and genuine that, after a pause, I answered him fully.

'Biro, this is a great problem. As you know, I'm deeply fond of both Erika and Mina. Both are fine, strong, affectionate girls who help to keep me in peak condition. But to marry Mina might involve a divorce – and it is unthinkable that I, Count Dracula, should ever be arraigned and questioned in an English court like some commoner.'

Biro nodded in reluctant agreement.

'And then, Erika. True, her father is a Master at Eton College; perfectly respectable people but not of the background and breeding that I must require. I am a Szekely, a Dracula of princely blood; to marry a mere pedagogue's daughter ...'

Biro, dear fellow, again nodded his head sadly, seeing no easy way out of my predicament.

October 21st

I write this entry in astonishment and generally with happiness.

The estate itself is marvellously restored. Crops stand again, herds and flocks are re-established, it is almost as though Tomas and Niklaus and the trade unions had never been as prosperity begins to return. This is the work of my wonderful Uncle and the new overseer, Arapad Howkoja, a dull, able, hardworking man who, fortunately, seems to pay no regard to his tiresome wife.

But Mr Candler, who welcomed me briskly, has wrought an even greater transformation. Entry to the long Castle drive is now under an arch which boldly announces 'Hotel Dracula', and then gives some details of *en pension* and bed-and-breakfast terms. The Great Black Lake, hard by the wolf pens, was always somewhat gloomy and my revered Father at one time considered populating it with alligators, creatures of whom he was always fond. But now the darker surrounding trees have been felled, the lakeside sedge cleared and a kind of beach made on the north side; bright-painted little bathing cabins dot this shore, a raft bobs in the water nearby, and gay-coloured canoes lie on the strand ready for use. Biro looked in amazement at a burly man in a bathing costume and cap who had 'Life Guard' embroidered across his chest: 'That's my cousin Fyodor, and I'll swear he can't swim a stroke. Come to think of it, he's never even had a bath.'

The wolf pens have been moved to a different position, and are now so aranged that the tourists can examine them closely yet safely. Many of the wolves seemed to have a reddish stain on their jowls and, impulsively, I exclaimed, 'Good gracious, is that blood?'

One old wolf, who recognised me, looked up and explained, 'That's what the customers are meant to think. It isn't blood of course, but they're putting a lot of betel nut in our food. Quite tasty, really.'

To the left in the Great Hall now lay a desk marked Reception.

The care of this was one of the duties shared by Trandafira, Vlastimila and Pavola now smartly uniformed and wearing maids' bonnets which said 'Candler's Dandier'. (I think these new Americanisms will ruin the language.)

'Dear girls,' said Mr Candler, patting Vlastimila fondly, 'their command of English has been such a help.'

I was momentarily puzzled.

'You had a Mr Brute here, if you remember, a prizefighter. English was among the things he taught these excellent girls.'

Pavola beamed at him and said, 'Cor strewth, stone the bleedin' crows, yus;' in accents which recalled dear 'Enery perfectly to mind.

To the right was a desk with a sign, 'Bell Sergeant', where our beloved old Footescu sat in a very new uniform and a very old chair. Each time I meet Footescu I fear it must be the last – I've felt this for a decade now – so our reunion was most affectionate. As I helped him to sit down again, I asked what the sign meant. Mr Candler seemed to take the sense of my question for he interposed hastily: 'You see, Count, there's a snappy new American term for a head porter – comes from New York – they call him the Bell Captain. But we couldn't really see Footescu as a captain of anything, so we compromised on Bell Sergeant.'

Upstairs, the huge bedrooms, in which the vast canopied beds had taken up only a tiny proportion of the space, had been converted into small neat identical rooms with comfortably mattressed beds. These rooms were much lighter too, and I realised that, apart from a good deal of wall washing and new paint, for the first time in my remembrance the windows had been cleaned. Great advances had been made in bathroom and toilet arrangements: the sole disadvantage of this was the evident decline of our previously fecund rhubarb beds outside the west scullery door.

The Great Banqueting Hall, unused in my lifetime, now presented its wood floor gleaming and polished almost to danger point, and tables with cheerful checked cloths and shining cutlery. A burly gypsy violinist, in romantic silken blouse, bow and fiddle in hand, strode across the room. Biro said faintly: 'Cousin Fyodor again. Didn't know he could play a note.'

'But,' Mr Candler said proudly, 'we have our very best dinners in the dungeons. We make only a small extra charge for Dungeon Dinners —and they're very popular indeed.'

The dungeons looked different. They were indeed much cleaner, and the Great Dungeon, adjoining the primary Torture Chamber, where my respected Father had spent so much of his time, now had in it a long refectory table which glowed in the candlelight. The candles also showed, against the black stone walls, several racks, thumbscrews, branding irons, wheels, and an ingenious piece of wall equipment for limb snapping which an early Dracula invented and perfected. Round the walls stood great numbers of impaling poles.

'We used not to have all this stuff,' I said.

'I know. Isn't it splendid? So atmospheric, I got most of the newer items from your Uncle: can't speak highly enough of the help he's given.'

The tapering sharp-pointed poles all had a rusty brown tinge to them.

'That's not blood,' I said, being perceptive in this area.

Mr Candler looked disappointed. 'No, you're right. But after a lot of experiments with matt red paint, it's very like it. Most of our tourists are quite convinced it's human blood.'

A squat formidable lady came in and began to polish the long table.

I felt Biro stiffen, and asked, 'Who is she?'

Biro answered in a low voice, 'She's a sort of aunt of mine. She has bad asthma and a worse temper. I remember once when she hit me with a besom ... ' Instinctively, he stepped behind me. 'I don't know about that,' said Candler rather crossly, 'but she's Mrs Nemesklai and she's very important for our Dungeon Dinners.'

'What does she do?' asked Biro, still apprehensive.

'Several things. First of all she makes the candles gutter. She has large foot bellows behind that pillar, and she blows them from time to time to give a guttering effect: guttering candles are essential for Dungeon Dinners. Then behind another pillar we've got some old chains and as the evening wears on she rattles them now and again. And she groans.'

'It's her asthma,' said Biro.

'That could be. I can only say that we had a number of auditions, and Mrs Nemesklai was by far the best wheezer and groaner. It's very atmospheric, and we're very glad to have her.'

Mr Candler looked extremely serious as he turned to us and continued, 'And then there's the Vampires.'

Biro and I stood stock still. I was glad of the deep shadows of the dungeon, for I felt the blood drain from my face.

'Yes, Vampires. There seems to be a strong belief that vampires, the Un-Dead who have a human appearance but can change into vampire bats bringing death and damnation to those they attack, live and thrive in this very region. Do you, Count, know anything of these legends?'

I said, very evenly, 'Of course. I was brought up with these absurd old wives' tales.'

'Old wives' tales they may be, but they have great pulling power. I believe we're going to be booked out next season, and I tell you it's this vampire business that boosts the bookings.'

'I'm so pleased to hear it.'

'So we tried to capture a few bats. As you know, there are some professional catchers round here; they try to get them for Walpurgis Night. But we couldn't get enough, so I've had these made up.'

Mr Candler took from his jacket pocket a small bit of soggy rubber, into which he blew vigorously. Immediately he had in his hand a balloon similitude of a vampire bat.

'These,' he said, 'are filled with some gas and then Mrs Nemesklai releases them just at the end of the dinner and it's most effective. We've had faintings, hysterics and one premature birth — Mrs Nemesklai does midwifery as well. The tourists absolutely love it.'

I congratulated him, and said that I thought that enough for

130

one day.

'Of course, of course,' said Mr Candler. 'We've one or two little problems as well, but I'll tell you of them tomorrow.'

October 22nd

Whilst it is good to be back at the Castle and sleeping in my own three-poster bed (Footescu has been promising repair since the mid-on post collapsed the day Paris fell to the Prussians) my sleep was unusually disturbed.

'I thought the first party of tourists had come and gone,' I asked Candler at breakfast.

'Indeed they have. Last night's noise wasn't tourists, it's journalists.'

'How do they come into it?'

'People like the Cooks and me haven't only created travel, but travel writers too. We brought several journalists on this first tour here – you could almost call it an inauguration – and most of them will write it up in the papers.'

'Do they pay their way?'

Mr Candler looked shocked: 'They're journalists. Of course they don't.'

'Why are they still here?'

'That's our current problem. All the rest were very well behaved and left with the tourists: just two stayed and won't go.'

'Biro and I could assist their departure?'

'They must go voluntarily. The press is always powerful and often malicious. Got to keep on the right side of 'em. Anyway, one of them's very nice, except that he's mad about woman's hockey.'

'You won't find that round here,' I said firmly.

'My dear Count, but you will – now. Tonight the local area semi-finals are between Floreseu and Boby, Saghy and Pullai. They are playing for the Eastgate – that's his name – the Eastgate Transylvanian Ladies' Hockey Trophy. Don't ask me how he got

131

the whole thing under way, equipment and all: pure force of fanaticism, I suppose.'

'Well, it's a harmless enough sport.'

'Count Dracula,' said Candler shaking his head, 'your life has indeed been sheltered. Let me tell you that as a consequence of the preliminary rounds the hospital at Bistritz is overflowing with patients with cracked heads and shins. They've had to requisition part of the Golden Krone Hotel nearby, just to find the bed space. And some of the more seriously wounded have been evacuated to the Hospital of St Joseph and Ste Marie in Buda-Pesth.'

I was shocked at the idea of such bloodshed.

'This hockey gives women the most extraordinary ideas. For example, according to Footescu, when Lubomir Hula took off his belt last Saturday night to thrash his wife – and Footescu says he's done this every Saturday night for the past ten years – she suddenly hit him over the head with her hockey stick. They don't know which has upset him more, the concussion or the shock of the totally unprovoked attack. And we need Lubomir here,' Mr Candler ended up a little anxiously, 'keeping his eye on the plumbing and the Castle sewers.'

I had finished breakfast, and hoped to stroll with Biro around the grounds, but Mr Candler went on. 'We need to get rid of Eastgate. Even more must we be rid of Jake Nobbs. He's the one making all the noise and trouble: keeps demanding that we send up more drink and some girls or he'll write bad things about us.'

'You don't — ?'

'He's been so drunk for days there'd be no point in sending girls anyway. And he rants away about starting a sort of National Union – of, I think, journalists – which would ensure they only worked a twelve-hour week, couldn't be sacked and spent the rest of the time in marches and protest rallies.'

'Nobbs sounds a nasty creature by any standards.'

'Yes. He is. Eastgate is quite agreeable. But both must go.'

My mind had been racing, and I announced, rising from the table, 'Both will be gone by this time tomorrow.'

132

October 23rd

Although I did not speak to Mr Candler this morning at breakfast, I could not but be gratified at the fresh respect in his eye. For, soon after first light the two journalists, Jake Nobbs in a crazy state of alcoholic terror, acquired a calèche and galloped, reckless and swaying, down the drive.

The veterinary doctor has been here today, as now is the time when he milks the bats in early preparation for Walpurgis Night. He prescribed and obtained for me a quantity of throat lozenges, of a strength comparable with K's own variety, but these have so far failed to restore my power of speech.

The cause of my loss of speech was my long duet with Lajos, the old wolf who, like Casanova, remembered me on my return. I collected him from the pen about midnight, transformed myself, and he and I then howled steadily outside the journalists' windows, sometimes in unison and sometimes harmonising, rather as they do in barber-shop singing. If Eastgate was comparatively unperturbed, Nobbs, especially after he had opened his casement and seen our crouched grey forms and burning amber eyes, fell into a state of infectious terror. Lajos seemed greatly to enjoy all this howling – for which I rewarded him with a special bonus – but my unaccustomed throat was much affected.

I passed a breakfast note to Mr Candler which red: 'Regret speechless from aphonia. Journalists now left, but as this was caused by organised wolf howling under windows, hope this will not bring adverse results.'

Mr Candler passed back a note (for the life of me I can't think why, since I am speechless but certainly not deaf) which read: 'Profound thanks for solving v. awkward problems. Probable write-up compaining wolf howlings should *double/treble* bookings for Castle Dracula.'

October 29th

During the journey back from my transformed Castle I had reflected, pleasurably, on the interview I intended to have with Jonathan Harker. The damaging evidence I now held against him would ensure both a return of the rental of which he sought to cheat me and the safety of my continuing connection with his Mina.

Harker came in and with an air of brisk formality paid me the balance of rent due from Madame Roza. 'And the rest, please,' I said.

I let him splutter away for a minute or so, watching his uneasiness grow, and then very quietly laid before him a copy of Mrs Roza's affidavit which Mr Dunning had obtained. He went blood-red, then white.

'This can mean professional ruin for you.'

He nodded: no words came.

'If you ever again cross me; if you ever go contrary to my wishes, I shall use this affidavit. Otherwise I shall merely retain it. Now pay me the balance you tried to steal, and go.'

Harker may now be a partner in his firm of attorneys, looking after the London business and scraping an acquaintanceship with some quite well connected people, but as he crept to the door he looked like a Moldavian peasant (Moldavian nobles treat their people very ill).

Mr Dunning had rapidly carried out my instructions and leased for me a small apartment in central London, in Dyott Street. So I immediately sent a note to Mina Harker, and after tea set off to meet her there. My spirits were high since my hold on her husband ensured that there could be no tiresome divorce proceedings, no question of the dignity of a Dracula being challenged in a court, nothing along the lines of the famous Sir Charles Mordaunt divorce case a few years earlier, the sordid details of which had given so many of my friends so much pleasure.

I bounded up the stairs of the Dyott Street apartment feeling at peace with the world. I threw open the drawing room door and almost immediately was struck on the right ear by a glazed china pig. A moment later an earthenware spaniel landed on my temple. I looked for the source of these missiles ... and my blood froze.

What I had feared — what Biro would have forestalled had he not been engaged in moving back to Piccadilly — had happened: Erika and Mina had coincided in the same apartment.

I surmised that each had quickly realised my relations with the other. Battle appeared to have been quickly joined: most of the furniture was overturned, Mina looked as if fresh from a violent ladies' hockey match, Erika as if from a Rugby scrum. Both were breathing heavily, looking extraordinarily attractive and in furious tempers — not, alas, any longer with each other, but with me.

It was deeply distressing to hear the epithets they launched at me: 'Rake! Betrayer! Ruffian! Vile seducer! Violator! Corruptor! Monster! Wolf!' (I started at this) 'Hellhound! Destroyer of innocence!'

It was no less distressing that they continued to hurl objects at me as well; worst of all was that both were infernally accurate. They might well have spent their formative years at coconut shies.

'Ladies, ladies,' I cried, 'my two dear ladies. I can see you are upset. But cannot we be reconciled? Cannot we three kiss and make up?'

'Never, never!' screamed Erika. 'Never after the way you've treated me. Faithful to you, I've been, although that nice Ensign Hooley has been after me like anything. Wish in that fight he'd knocked you flat,' she added, hurling a Benares brass tray, which nearly did.

'And I was so faithful to you,' she wailed again.

Voicing a small suspicion, I snapped, 'What about William Gordon-Cumming, then?'

Erika fell silent for a moment, but Mina said loudly and very

135

woundingly, 'Kiss and make up! With you! I'd sooner do it with my bloody husband.'

An aristocrat must accept defeat with grace. Bowing (to be more exact, ducking) I said, 'Dearest ladies, knowing you both has given me the greatest happiness. But now must be the time for us to part. Farewell to you both.'

I slammed the door behind me and went noisily down the stairs. Then I tiptoed up again and put my ear to the keyhole. They appeared to be comforting each other and to be set for a lifelong friendship (at least, I reflected, they'd had something in common).

Their voices, not individually distinguishable, were saying, 'Oh, he was lovely. Such a nice skin. Such strong white teeth. So lithe. Didn't he kiss well? Those beautiful, beautiful love bites.'

There were other comments which, although flattering, I prefer not to record. But they also seemed agreed and determined on one thing. 'We can't have him back. No, never. Too humiliating, it would be. A matter of pride. We girls *must* have our pride.'

Sadly, reflecting that pride in women is perhaps the deadliest of the seven great sins, I made my way to a pharmacist, bought a quantity of arnica, and went home.

October 30th

Biro was greatly concerned this morning at my contusions and fussed about with witch hazel and more arnica. But he would keep chattering happily about his forthcoming wedding, and I began to feel increasingly gloomy and frustrated: it was absurd that the good fellow's prospects should be so much brighter than my own.

Suddenly I said, 'Biro. Take a hansom this afternoon to Miss Lee Gan. Ask her if she will do me the honour of dining with me tonight. If she can, wait there and bring her back.'

She arrived looking delightful, and gave me the happiest of smiles. Excepting only my own (to judge from what I am told, as I have this allergy to mirrors), she must have the whitest teeth in the world. But her face changed when she saw my abrasions and immediately and with great gentleness she applied additional quantities of witch hazel and arnica.

We dined at the Café Royal. As we made our way to our private room we heard Oscar Wilde, who was sitting there plumply, surrounded by cronies, make one of his witticisms. A slightly drunk man lurched past, bumping into a marble-topped table – 'Where there's a swill there's a sway,' said Oscar.

Everyone laughed uproariously: I didn't think it all that amusing.

I cannot remember a more delightful dinner. It is not only that Nancy saved my life, but that she is lively, intelligent and entirely sympathetic. Looking at her neat, well-formed elegance I was reminded that by comparison Erika and Mina were hoydens.

'You move,' I said, 'like a princess. I wish you were one; it would be so romantic to have one's life saved by a princess.'

'Perhaps I am,' replied Nancy. 'My family always call me Princess. I was born here, you know, and my parents died when I was very small, but my sort-of-uncle who is our guardian says that my father's power and authority in the far province of

137

Liaoning were such that I truly should be called Princess. Jealousy and intrigue made him flee for his life but,' she added thoughtfully, 'some valuables seem to have accompanied his flight.'

I was deeply interested in all this and asked her a great many questions. Finally she said, 'so there it is. Certainly, nobody can prove that I'm a princess. But nobody can prove I'm not, either.'

'Do you mean,' I said slowly, 'that if, for example, your engagement should be announced in the *Morning Post* and *The Times* as Princess Nancy Lee Gan, none could gainsay it, nobody could dispute it?'

'Nobody.'

We rose to leave the private room. I slipped her cloak over her gold-silk shoulders, and ventured to kiss her, warmly and indeed with increasing warmth. She responded with a delightful directness.

'Will you return to Piccadilly before we take you home?' I asked. 'You can of course be secure in the knowledge that my most respectable housekeeper, Mrs Merry, is once again in residence.'

'Of course,' said Nancy. After a pause she added, 'It is yet more comforting that she must long since have gone to bed.'

October 31st

I woke late feeling astonishingly well and happy, despite the fact that some of my contusions had turned greenish.

Biro brought me coffee, rolls and Haemozade.

'Biro,' I asked cautiously, 'have you any knowledge of what happened last night?'

'I know exactly what happened, Master, and she is a delightful young lady.'

'I'm glad you think so.'

'If you will forgive me, sir, by far the most delightful of your several young ladies.'

I hummed a few staves from *Ruddigore*, my favourite Savoy opera.

'Do you know, Biro, I had intended to make an – an approach to Miss Lee Gan last night. But I think – I'm almost sure – that she had already decided on the same course. Imagine that.'

'The biter bit,' said Biro, adding 'Sorry, Master,' very hastily indeed.

I have virtually made my decision that Nancy shall be my betrothed. A wedding between a Dracula, of princely blood, and a beautiful Chinese girl similarly enriched seems socially excellent. Further, although I am of the Un-Dead, I feel the most lively affection and desire for her. Before breakfast was done I had dispatched Biro poste-haste across Europe to Uncle Vlad with an explanatory message and a request for his approval.

November 1st

I took Nancy to see dear Mr Drummond whose opinions I so greatly value. At first he was disconcerted ('After all, Dracula,' he said later, 'she is – well – *foreign*') but in no time at all she had captivated him and he was teaching her under-arm bowling. I was delighted when he pronounced decisively, 'A delightful young lady. You've done well. Splendid how she gets her fingers on the seam of the ball.'

I also arranged for Roy Dracula to lunch with Nancy and me, for I regard him as an excellent arbiter of taste. If I can persuade dear Crispin Bell-Mountain up from the Cotswolds to meet her and he too approves, then I shall know my decision is right and my judgement unchallengeable. I shall not introduce her to Bram Stoker: my enthusiasm for that jolly Irishman has waned since I heard a strong rumour that he is writing a book about me.

November 2nd

The meal with Roy — it was at Romano's — was slightly marred by the arrival of Alfred Austin, who came across to our table. 'My dear people' he said, 'my great epic poem is almost complete: soon it will be published and there for the world to admire. And to buy,' he added.

Roy made encouraging noises. He is very good at making these noises, not actually saying anything but giving a strong illusion of interest. Perhaps he should enter political life.

'Yes,' said Austin, 'I've dwelt at some length on the good Prince Consort. Always judicious, you know. Here's an extraordinarily dramatic piece I wrote about his illness:

Across the wire th' electric message came
He is no better he is much the same.'

Roy said that it had him sitting on the edge of his chair.
'And then after his sad demise:

The Prince to be a Consort bravely tried
And people were quite sorry when he died.'

Mr Austin fell into such a paroxysm of grieving emotion at this that the head waiter came over anxiously. Nancy poured him a glass of excellent dry white wine: Roy rapidly substituted for it a tumbler of cold water.

'And so,' Austin continued, 'the whole great British epic comes almost to the present day, comes to the death of Disraeli. Pray, listen:

Across the globe all sorts of people daily
Deplore the sad demise of poor Disraeli.'

His voice choked at the end of this couplet, and I feared that there would be another outburst. But at that point a waiter came up and told us that the beefsteak, kidney and oyster pie was ready, and Mr Austin mopped his eyes and returned rapidly to his table.

Roy asked Nancy what she thought of Austin's verse; she replied politely that she prefered Ku K'ai Wang and Tennyson. I said nothing. I had never heard of the former but had attended a reading by Tennyson and found his sonorous honking Lincolnshire voice quite intolerable. At the end of the lunch Roy leaned over and whispered to me: 'An absolutely delicious gal. Good enough to eat.'

November 9th

Yesterday was so filled with exciting turns of fate and fortune that it is only now that I can write it all down. First a weary Biro bought a letter from my Uncle Vlad, giving his unstinted approval to a unison with a Chinese princess. He wrote, 'I'm sure she will have a wide and valuable knowledge of Tortures.'

Then I went straightway to a little jeweller (I got his name from Sir John Maple who is also in trade) and bought a sapphire-and-diamond engagement ring, the sapphire being of excellent colour and the diamonds very large. In some haste – for now that I'd made my decision I wished to declare it – I made my way to Nancy's house, went up to her room and said without more ado: 'Nancy, my dearest, I have decided that we shall be betrothed. Here is my betrothal ring. Please put it on.'

Women are, increasingly, curious creatures. Sometimes I feel it is the fault of education. I had expected an explosion of happiness, delight and gratitude. What she in fact said was: '*You've* decided that we're betrothed, have you? And what about *me*? What have I decided? I haven't decided anything. And why haven't I decided anything? Because – ' I never realised she could develop so strong a voice – 'I damned well haven't been asked!'

Then there was a singing note just by my right ear, similar I would think to a soldier receiving the attentions of an enemy marksman, which was made by my betrothal ring whistling past at very high speed. I bowed and left the room, closing the door gently. It was hard to believe that her small and exquisite body could generate the fearful howls that followed me through the hall.

A note awaited me at 347 Piccadilly. I was so dazed that it took two readings for me to realise that K was summoning me most urgently. I hastened to Goodwin's Court.

'Right, Dracula, sit down,' said K. He was using his quiet voice. I sat down between Mr Drummond and Stock.

'This is a quick in-and-out mission, and it needs the lingo. Background: Prince Milan of Serbia – heard of the fellow?'

'I've met him. Didn't like him. The Obrenovitches tend to be arrogant.'

K gave me a surprised look. 'Then d'you know his half-brother, Prince Ranko?'

'Saw him as a baby. He's only about twelve now: either a half-brother or a by-blow.'

'But still an Obrenovitch. Still commanding romantic loyalty and affection and all that.'

I nodded, although I don't care for the family.

'Right. We and the Austrians don't like Milan; pro-Russian, pro-Slav, unreliable. If we got him removed, Ranko would make a popular substitute. Boy's virtually a prisoner in Kaledan Castle, bit north of Beograd.'

'I've been there.'

'Good. We're going to get him out before Milan has him killed; keep him safe in case he comes in useful. We'll do it by using the lingo and a very clever idea I've had — '

Mr Drummond stirred restively.

' – a clever idea Drummond and I had. Based on what's goin' on at your own Castle now.'

'How do you mean?'

'No more now. Full details when you get there.'

'Where?'

K took one of his dreadful lozenges and suddenly bawled, 'A little pension called the Ceterichi in Cluj. Be there Friday night: you'll be contacted. Shall I repeat that?'

'No, thank you.'

K repeated it, even more loudly.

'Now, Dracula,' K resumed, speaking quietly and quickly, 'private word with you.'

Mr Drummond and Stock rose, bade Miss Buckle a cheerful good day in the outer office and clattered out into the little alley.

'Much appreciate your loyalty. Lot of chaps would have backed off at a time like this.'

'Like what?'

'Getting married. Looks very important at the time. Remember getting married myself.'

He shivered slightly, paused to drink a glass of port, and went rapidly on: 'Want to show our appreciation. In all quarters. Highest quarters. Very highest quarters: read this.'

Count Dracula of Transylvania

Your work for our country has reached our ears – the Queen is *much* interested and *enchanted* to learn of your deeds! Strange are the dispensations of Providence that *you* – not by BIRTH English – should be so *embrouillé* in our affairs!!

If the Queen was a man (!) she would be *proud* to act as you have against those *horrid* Russians, many half-*mad* firebrands, whose word one *cannot* TRUST!

'Britons *never* will be Slaves' remains our Motto – you have gained a Wreath of Laurels ensuring this – and the Queen will soon despatch a TOKEN to you *comme souvenir*.

Formal recognition – of your lofty service – will be made, but here the Queen writes *personally* ... in your exploits you must have thought – deeply – of the TEXT on which I *doat* (Amos Ch. 4, v. 12) 'Prepare to meet thy God, O Israel'.

Victoria R.I.

I was overpowered with pleasure. I did not know what to say.

'And more. When you've got the boy Ranko out of Serbia, Drummond and Stock will take him off your hands the other side of the frontier. Before that Drummond will escort your girl – ideal girl he says she is – to Castle Dracula. Join her there when you've finished the mission. Have some furlough. Enjoy yourselves.'

K closed his left eye in a dreadful wink.

'But, but … ' I began helplessly.

'No buts. All arranged. Drummond's at your girl's house by now, tellin' her. Now, don't thank me – ' K raised his hand – 'don't thank me: wanted to show practical appreciation. Be off now. The password's Mendez.'

The interview was over. I returned bewildered to Piccadilly, bade Biro pack for a dawn departure, and went early to bed in a condition of total confusion.

November 10th

It must have been some two hours later when I was awakened by a commotion at my door. It was Biro, gently but firmly trying to prevent someone from entering my bedroom. His efforts failed, for the door was flung open and Nancy rushed into the room. 'Mr Drummond says you are going off to do something dangerous and I think you might be killed and it would be *awful* if we'd parted in anger.'

The world seemed to be getting increasingly unpredictable but I agreed cautiously that it would.

'And you thinking I don't love you and won't marry you. And I do and I will if you'd ask me. But you didn't ask me, you just told me. Like – like giving patronage to a butcher.'

There was nothing for it. I buttoned up my Chinese silk pyjamas, rolled from my bed, plumped on my knees and said, 'Dear Miss Lee Gan – dear, dear Nancy, will you please, please, consider doing me the honour of becoming my wife?'

144

At this she burst into howls even louder than earlier in the day. But this time, since they were howls of happiness, they had a quite different timbre.

Nancy was still sleeping when Biro and I left quietly just before dawn. Her betrothal ring – sparkling very brilliantly on her finger because she had soaked it in gin throughout the day – had left a small abrasion in my lumbar area.

Mr Drummond was in the hansom outside, reliable and comforting, although I wished he would delay the smoking of his first pipe of the day until later. As we rattled towards Victoria he said, 'Change of plan. Don't go to Cluj Friday night, go to Arad Thursday night: the pension Draganescu in Arad, and ask for our man there, Trandafir Bobu.'

'K changed his plans on a previous mission,' I said. 'The bits he shouts at me particularly loudly, he always seems to have second thoughts on.'

Mr Drummond chuckled. 'No, no. You see, we don't think that they know that we know that they know K's place in Goodwin's Court. Whenever they think there's anything afoot they have people outside, loitering and listening. And when K shouts, he wants them to hear – to hear wrong information.'

And they say that the English are invariably stupid.

'You have to remember,' Drummond continued sombrely, 'that Russian purse-strings are long, Van Helsing is richly supplied with money – throughout Europe he can buy men to do his fell work.'

We parted at Victoria with a short, firm handclasp.

November 17th

I write down these events while they are yet fresh in my mind. Last night we lay in a modest, rather dirty inn almost under the forbidden walls of Kaledan Castle.

By 'we' I mean a carriage-load of tourists, ostensibly of Mr Candler's Transylvanian tourists, who, as an 'extra', are visiting this castle. Bobu, their leader, who declared himself at the frontier as the tour guide and interpreter, tells me that money has passed and full permission been given by the Castle authorities, who appear to keep young Ranko under a loose house arrest.

This morning we put our plan into action. Our coach drove past the lodge at the main gates – we were checked by armed men as we passed, but I noticed that small side entrances in the walls were unguarded – and we spilled out in the Castle courtyard. We had guide books and sketch pads (Biro was in his element here); we wandered like the veriest tourists through the Castle and its grounds. We numbered seven, and that included Bobu's son, wearing a tweed hat resembling that of my curious acquaintance Sherlock Holmes, which would have been large on Holmes and greatly obscured the lad's face, and a vivid green jacket.

It was Bobu who found Ranko. He was playing alone in a room, apparently unguarded. We alerted our group to return to the coach, Bobu's son gave me his hat and jacket and slipped away through a side gate, Bobu and I entered Ranko's room and before the boy could speak the chloroform pad was over his face.

'Come, come, Ludovic, my son,' shouted Bobu loudly as he and I, each holding an arm, bundled the boy in the huge tweed hat and bright green jacket into the coach, 'I told you if you didn't come when time was up we'd carry you, you naughty boy.'

Past the lodge gates – they barely glanced at us – we paused only to pick up the real Ludovic, and set our coach rumbling towards the frontier.

At this point Ranko came round: we stopped the coach while he was sick. I explained to him that we were saving his life: he did not appear particularly grateful and was sick again. As we lumbered on, the most fearful stench assailed us; we stopped again but precious minutes passed before, handkerchiefs to our noses, we were able to resume our seats. A league or two more, and Ludovic gave a wild scream and pointed to the floor: a black-and white barred snake moved and writhed venomously there, and two of our party injured themselves as they leaped from the moving coach. On cautious inspection the snake proved to be made of india-rubber.

I looked suspiciously at Prince Ranko. The boy looked back at me with large round innocent eyes.

'Have you something to do with this?' I demanded.

'Oh no,' he cried, 'of course not. You are my friends – saving my life. Here, please, have these; I took them from my tutor's desk this morning.'

He produced a packet of cigarettes. I declined his offer; my companions accepted; our driver, who was having a difficult time of it, lit up and inhaled with deep satisfaction.

The series of explosions came about two minutes later. All the cigarettes blew up at about the same time: the explosion in the driver's face entirely unnerved him. It startled the horses, too: the coach left the rough road for the rocky ditch, and the last of the ensuing noises was a ferocious crash which suggested that a wheel had broken off.

The shaken silence in which we all sat was broken by peals of laughter from Ranko. 'All my Tricks worked,' he shouted. 'Every one of the Tricks worked perfectly. You should have seen your faces.'

I seized the boy, removed his green jacket and searched the capacious pockets of his own coat beneath.

'At least,' I said, removing a packet marked Itching Powder, 'there's one trick you haven't used.'

'I have, too,' cried Ranko. 'I put it down that man Bobu's trousers just now. It'll start to work soon.'

Bobu grabbed at Ranko. Ranko bit him.

'Bobu,' I said with restraint, 'will you go out and consider the damage to our vehicle while I talk to the young Prince.'

I spanked Ranko for some while, at the same time explaining to him the realities of the situation. Bobu returned. 'The repairs,' he said grimly, 'will take twenty-four hours. Horsemen will be ahead of us.'

November 18th

We completed our repairs today and edged north-westwards along small roads and tracks (even the best Serbian roads are quite different from Watling Street), aiming to cross the frontier at some deserted point. At dusk we were near: our narrow road ran through a ravine and then straight for a few hundred metres to the border and safety. We stopped and looked towards the ravine, its western crest sharp against the dying winter sun. Biro said quickly, 'Master, there are men there.'

Despite Bobu's protests, I insisted that I would deal with this situation. 'You'll never climb that track of rock and scree without being heard, and then they'll kill you.' Only Biro, guessing at what I planned, did not seek to dissuade me.

I transformed to a wolf as soon as I started up the track. It was a long climb: even four-footed and placing my paws with delicacy it was hard to be silent. But I reached the crest and stood behind the enemy. There were six of them, their rifles at the ready as they looked over the edge at the ribbon of the road below, now white in the early moonlight. One of the men, evidently the NCO in charge, said very deliberately, 'Remember, we kill them all. Especially, we kill the boy. And afterwards we say his death was an unfortunate accident. Understand?'

I transformed again, and spoke. I have been told that my voice can have a quality of menace. Generally that idea is quite ridiculous, but I achieved menace this time. 'Throw your rifles over the crest. Before we kill you. Don't look round.'

One soldier half looked back at me. I instantly fired my revolver in his direction: I still don't understand this weapon but it went off with a most satisfactory noise. He threw his rifle down immediately; the others followed suit.

'Down the track,' I commanded.

They set off before me, but too slowly and grudgingly. I changed back to wolf form and, although I knew I might later suffer some loss of voice, gave a series of full-blooded howls.

The effect was galvanic. Six wretched creatures, in a state of exhausted terror, tumbled and stumbled to the bottom of the track. My companions took and donned their uniforms, leaving them in their deplorable underclothes. We passed across the frontier with no more than a sleepy hail.

As our coach rolled on to safety, and towards the Arad road, we climbed a steady gradient to a pass. We paused: the white ribbon of road emerging from the ravine was now ten miles distant, but still brightly moonlit. On it horses and a great cloud of dust now appeared; it looked like a half-squadron of Prince Milan's cavalry. Would they, I wonder, have taken us prisoner or butchered us on the spot?

We all shook hands. We were so relieved that Bobu even shook hands with Ranko. 'But don't you ever put itching powder on me again.'

Ranko, who had formed a close alliance with Ludovic, looked up thoughtfully. 'I wonder what new Tricks I'll find in London.'

November 24th

As we topped the Borgo Pass I looked around with satisfaction. The fields were again well cultivated and the stock strong, as though SODU had never been. I had faced actual poverty but wealth was returning – increased even, with Mr Candler's tourist venture at my Castle. Ahead lay my home, and within it my betrothed.

As planned, I had handed Ranko over to Mr Drummond and Stock soon after we'd crossed the border, with the comfortable feeling that K's approbation, and indeed that even higher approval, had again been fairly earned. To my great pleasure, Ranko had kept one Trick up his sleeve, terrifying Stock with an excellent similitude of an astonishingly large and hairy spider.

I looked back and these agreeable thoughts were shattered. Several calèches, indeed a fleet of calèches, were following Biro and me along the lonely dusty road. Furiously driven, they were gaining on us. Instantly I divined that their intention was hostile: I strained my eyes at the figure in the leading vehicle, and my lips framed the name – Van Helsing. If I had thought of this evil creature at all during the past few days, it was of him vainly waiting in Cluj; at best a socially insupportable town. Clearly I had made a mistake, and the extent of my error appalled me.

For Van Helsing had with him at least ten ruffians (Drummond was right about the length of Russian purse-strings) and all would be armed. Within the Castle, towards which I was now galloping wildly, there would be very few people. Old Footescu would be dozing and talking fitfully to himself. Trandafira, Vlastimila and Pavola would be about the place; I hoped that their resistance to death would at least be sturdier than to the fate worse than death. There might be one or two women cleaning up the Dungeon Dining Room – the very last tourists of the season would have left some days earlier – but that was the total of possible defenders. Except of course – I felt as though a dagger were in my heart – for my darling Nancy. Considering what he had suffered at my hands, and from Nancy's brother's instruments, I realised with mounting desperation that Van Helsing would assuredly kill us both.

I leaped from the calèche and bounded up the balustraded steps. Footescu, huddled shapelessly, sat inside the great doors.

'Have you a pistol?' I cried, unceremoniously.

'Yes, Master.' He beamed and with surprising speed took from a drawer a formidable-looking revolver. He pointed it at a chandelier and jerked the trigger. A thin jet of water emerged. I groaned.

'Footescu,' I shouted, 'any second some enemies, cruel, murderous men, will come through the door. Hide now, keep your head down, you may save your skin.'

I rushed up the main staircase. At the top Nancy appeared, welcoming and more beautiful than ever. Biro and I ran to her. There was scarcely time for explanation, for already the enemy was at the door.

We tried to fight, but in vain. We fled from room to room, I fired the remaining shots in my revolver, but always wide of the mark (it is curious that I am perfectly sound on a grouse moor yet uesless with a revolver); finally we were cornered, standing by the opened casement window of the Banqueting Hall – the very window from which I had made my first proving flight with Uncle Vlad.

Even at this stage I could have transformed and fluttered away: I instantly dismissed this course of action as impossible for a Transylvanian nobleman and an old Balliol man. Nancy thrust her firm little hand into mine, four ruffians covered us, Van Helsing walked slowly towards us, revolver in hand.

'In case you should think of a dramatic leap through the casement,' he said, moving leisurely round till he stood with his back to the window, 'I have plans for you to die in a lengthier and more traditional way.'

Usually his menacing tones were all too distinct. Now I had some difficulty in understanding him, until I realised that his new and tombstone-white false teeth were giving him trouble. Nancy realised it, too: 'Oh, Mr Van Helsing, what you need is "Dentadhere". It works wonders with new dentures. My brother could get you good supplies at a reduced rate. It would make you feel quite different.'

I think Van Helsing tried to say, 'My feelings and intentions are unlikely to change,' but his teeth came adrift again in mid-sentence.

'You poor man, you'd do better to take them out – wouldn't he be much more comfortable if he took them out?' she appealed to his henchman.

I translated for their benefit, and a fierce debate developed among them, the majority view being that he should probably leave them in.

'Enough,' Van Helsing gave a fierce muffled roar. 'We'll keep your girl and your servant here, where they'll die quickly, and take you to the Torture Chambers — '

'How do you know I've got Torture Chambers?' I demanded.

'I've read Mr Candler's prospectus. And in those chambers you'll die very slowly, very slowly indeed.'

At this point we were interrupted by the entry of some ladies; about sixty of them it proved subsequently. They came in laughing and chattering in a brisk body. One of Van Helsing's men tried to stop them, and reeled back holding an arm numbed by a blow from a parrot-head umbrella.

'Young man,' said one of the ladies sternly, 'I'd allow nobody in Oswaldtwistle to lay hands on me like that, and I'm not going to drop the standards of Oswaldtwistle just because I'm on holiday.'

The ladies surged remorselessly across the room.

'That Mr Candler's organised it all so well.'

'I don't know about that,' said another lady, 'delayed for a week in going back. We don't call that good organising in Bacup.'

'But it wasn't his fault. And it's grand having the extra week. And everything's so, well, realistic.'

'And you must be the owner, Count Dracula himself,' cried yet another lady suddenly.

'Indeed, madam, I am.'

'Honoured to meet you, Count,' she said, curtseying. I noticed that several other ladies bobbed to me: Lancashire is evidently a courteous county.

Van Helsing now began to shout very loudly and threateningly. But what with the general hubbub and his having kept his teeth in, the ladies were unable to understand what he was saying.

They crowded towards him to enquire. He retreated a pace or two – and, arms wide-stretched, fell backwards out of the window. A moment's frozen silence was followed by a single dreadful shriek. I leaped to the casement.

In the courtyard immediately below the window stood a serried row of impaling poles, and one of these now bore Van Helsing as its grisly burden. The impalement appeared to be technically perfect: even Uncle Vlad's personal supervision could have effected little improvement.

The ladies watched fascinated for a while.

'That Mr Candler's so clever. It's so realistic. You could really think it was real blood.'

There was some argument here, with a lady from Boggart Hole Clough maintaining that the blood on the body was far too bright to be the real thing. Then they went off to have cups of tea, taking Van Helsing's henchmen a little doubtfully with them. Biro followed them discreetly.

Nancy and I were alone: we embraced with fervour. As I contrasted the ebbing evil on the pole outside and the goodness and happiness which my arms now safely encircled, I thought to myself – I almost shouted it at the top of my voice – 'It's great, it's great, it's great to be Un-Dead!'